I0653208

COLONY
COLLAPSE

A Lazy Fascist Original

Lazy Fascist Press
An Imprint of Eraserhead Press
205 NE Bryant Street
Portland, Oregon 97211

www.lazyfascistpress.com

ISBN: 978-1-62105-080-3

Cover design by Matthew Revert
www.matthewrevert.com

Thanks to the following journals and anthologies for publishing sections of this book in their early iterations: *Apt, Big Lucks, Bending Light Into Verse, The Brooklyn Rail, Black Warrior Review, The Chattahoochee Review, Elimae, Everyday Genius, Fairy Tale Review, The Fiddleback, Ghost Ocean, Housefire, Kill Author, Midwestern Gothic, Precipitate, Redivider, Trnsfr, The Way We Sleep*

Printed in the USA.

COLONY COLLAPSE

J. A. TYLER

[the first house]

In these woods my brother handed me a note. A white paper sea sailing a black ship. I said to my brother *What does this mean?* and he said *There are no words* and I repeated *There are no words* but he was already a deer running back into the lake of these woods. A rabbit crossed from trunk to trunk, a bird from one umbrella of branches to another. My brother's note cried out my dying. A single black dot on a square of white meant that I was deathly, and my brother was a deer again, turning tail. My feet were hooves, but I could not chase down his reasons.

I started the search for my brother by building a house. With an axe I chopped down trees. I cut the limbs from their bodies. I shaved the stick-arms of their children. I used a saw to make each branch smaller. I sectioned the trunks into pieces. I notched and angled. I planed. I laid them in stacks until the stacks made walls, and I made walls until the house had four. I forged a roof. I covered the roof in evergreen and moss. I covered the roof in mud and sod. I covered the roof until there was a house to live in. When the first snow came I built a chimney. When the first rain came I fashioned gutters. With the first bout of sun, the cabin swollen in heat, I walked outside naked, my body coated in honey, and I waited for the bears to come.

The bears never came, only ants and gnats, flies buzzing. I lay prostrate in the meadow, flowers bending towards my elbows, a sky shining. There was the roll of ocean somewhere in the wind, and the tinkling of music from chimed pipes hung on the front porch of the house I had built. The bears were not as I had imagined, hungry for honeyed-skin, even with the sadness that comes of dying. There were no bears, and I woke with a coating of honey, a shell of a body on my body.

I wanted another chance to speak with my deer-brother, to have a new note clean white, one without black dying. While I waited I made jam, because mashing fruit with hands is an early kind of religion. I picked from the hills, washed their skins in rain. Inside the house I made jam. I sank them slowly in boiling sugar and pulped it all cool with fingers. I made raspberry and blueberry and blackberry jam. I ate the jam on biscuits. I served myself on plates of sky. I jammed biscuits, all my hope in what had come before.

When the first fox found my house, this fox with those eyes, he paced in my purview, watched me watching him, but there was no brother inside. This fox was not a brother. This fox had muscles and bloodied paws but was skittish of the walls I had constructed, scared of the invention of brother-living within his woods. So the fox bared his teeth and slunk back into the woods. I watched his tail go. He carried the darkness with him, constant night on his back, spreading pitch skies.

But tomorrow he came again to pace. Tomorrow he stood to watch, to revisit, this fox. Tomorrow after tomorrow he came until he laid a stick on the grass at my feet, at the doorstep, a jammed biscuit in my hand. I took the stick and tossed it away, out to the edges, past and into the darkness. This was a fox full of envy, jealous of hands. At the tree line's silky dusk, blood red paws in the strains of a forest tearing his next meat, that fox who was not my brother filled with quiet violence, was hooded by the darkness on his back.

There was snow, there was rain, there was sun again. And again I poured honey and went to the bears. And again the bears did not come. And again my body was a shell of a body, a thicket of new bones. And again I watched birds scatter from branches, and I went back to a house, and I made jam to writhe on biscuits, and I waited for the clean white of a different deer-brother's message.

But during the longest night, a second fox brought me a plug of sun in his mouth, set it in the grass grown around my feet. This was a softened fox, striding wide with soft paws. This fox felt like a brother, deer playing forest tag, running on mountains. This second fox was different from the first because he loved me, I could see it in his fur. We played up and through the trees. And with this second fox there was always light, always sun, and I forgot for a decade that I was dying. This second fox licked my face, I stroked his mane, and we pretended to find the brothers in each other. He nuzzled his fur on my leg, and the house around us shuttered with wealth.

This second fox became a part of me. This second fox held a piece of brotherhood that I needed. This second fox, we played, and then I opened his skin to see how it feels to be both inside of and settled beneath someone. I stabbed and gutted and skinned him. Wrapped in this second fox's hide, I had a new understanding of love. I made his bones into a crucifix, into a window frame, into a knife for opening wounds. I smeared a biscuit with fox-blood and ate, the two of us finally talking about what it means to survive.

Then another snow and another rain and another bout of sun. There was jam and there were biscuits. Birds in branches. Rabbits running from log to bush. The clouds hung above and I ignored the want to pour honey on my arms and raise them up. Instead I slept in the second fox's fur, melted into it, watched through the fox-bone window frame at the first fox approaching.

The first fox saw me wearing the second fox's skin, how I had slit open his belly and let all of the insides out. The first fox saw me wearing what had been his fellow fox, this furred life that once was his, and he could no longer resist the desire to step across my threshold. He entered my first house. He entered my first house and he stood on the floor that I had built from forest and sweat, and I plunged into his fox head the knife made from his fellow fox's bones. I held it downward until the first fox was quiet, until I could no longer hear him crying *Brother, brother.*

Inside of that first house I skinned the first fox of his jealousy, showed him that a brother is only for as long as a brother can be. I skinned the second fox of his hide, and the first fox crumbled. There was no more envy left for hands. And with the second fox's fur hiding my own brother-less body, and the first fox tangled in grief near the chimney, his head bowing as a branch gathering snow, I set fire to the first house, and all of us inside. We burned until ash and cinder ballooned up to the sky, these fox-brothers flaming away, a deer-brother running back into a maze of lost.

In these woods there is always the building up and burning down. In these woods fire reaches out with arms. In these woods I wore a fox hide to hide in, to skirt my own deer-brother's belief in death.

In these woods, I pretend escape. In these woods, we forget how to be brothers. In these woods, I build and burn houses until I can understand again what it means to live.

[the second house]

I built a second house over the mountains, in another meadow, away from the first where the sun shone and foxes came. Away from where I burned down for the first time. An opposite side where flowers are glaciers, where birds walk and rabbits curl around trees. With an axe and a saw and trees cut down to make four walls, I built a doorstep. I built a chimney for the snowfall and gutters for the rain and I scavenged honey from knotted holes to coat my nakedness, to feed the bears my body.

The second house was more a dreamscape than a life, bears knowing what it means to pretend, bears understanding that we are never to become children again, that the first house must be burnt to the grass beneath our feet before we can move on to bigger moments.

Underneath one answer is another, bear after bear always said.

Inside my second fox's scorched skin I watched glaciers melt towards me, in my second house, thinking always of dying, of what it means to end, my arms covered in fox-fur, my head peaked with the second fox's fuzzed skull, my fox-brother's worn-out crown.

In the second house I learned card tricks. And though a bear is not a brother, one came to watch me play, to be fooled in the riot of my magic, and I learned to memorize what it looked like in his bear's eyes when he pulled the queen of hearts or the ace of spades or the two of diamonds. I learned what it smelled like when he exhaled the six of clubs or the four of spades or the jack of hearts. The bear was astonished when I would say *Is this your card?* and it was. I memorized them all, fifty-two expressions on his bear face, fifty-two spectacles, fifty-two ways of knowing how it is to look inward. And my way with tricks kept that bear coming back, the perfect memorization of his being, though it was no replacement for my deer-brother, whom I hadn't seen in lifetimes.

Glaciers were slanting towards this second house and the bear was back day after day, my tricks soothing what was stuck-swollen on his bear tongue. His calling out *Brother?* and my cards coming up king of diamonds.

The bear believed I was a fox magician. I only wanted to believe that I wasn't dead. I only wanted to believe I hadn't done everything wrong in the secret living that had always taken place before I was lost in these woods.

My brother, on the edge of the forest, before I had built the first or the second house, before I had killed the first or skinned the second fox, he was a messenger, handing me a single black dot on a slip of paper. My deer-brother, handing out my dying.

I built the second house with a chimney, and even with its burning logs and the second-fox's fur, I was never beyond the feeling of deathly cold. There were blankets, but they were filled with death, and the nieces' eyes that snowed them down were a blackness I couldn't face.

That second house was more coffin than living.

When I grew weary of the cards, I moved to other magic for the bear who was not my brother. I went to sawing in half, to disappearances, to levitations, but he only wanted me to call cards. And I was too bored of cards to continue, so we became simply two posts on opposite ends of a line, drying a quilt between us, the wind coming down from a forested mountain, shale walls and frost, both of us colder each night.

There was hunger in my fists and in the bear's paws, and we sat together dying. Neither of us saying a word, the sun outside always lit yet no warmth to guide us into speaking.

Then the bear took to carving pictures on my wooden walls, and his pictures were so grand that I let him. They were masterpieces of sharpened claws. They were lovely with ease and sprawled across my second house, my heart rendered into walls and ceiling and floor. And the bear only looking up at me when I said *Is this your card?* Our glaciers were melting.

I shared my honey with the bear, and the bear shared his claws with me, playing so rough that I was days bleeding and bones crushed. He was a bear, not a brother, and there has never been such gouging play in a deer's hooves.

But this second house was more a hollow than a home, and the bear grew as restless with our playing as I had with the cards. To a bear, tearing open a brother is like back-patting, and both of us wanted more than a pretend herd of miscellaneous parts. My second-fox's skin was only a covering, and my scepter not a victory.

I begged him to finish the work, his mural, what he had been making through the years, a forest-scape that looked like where my brother was, in a deer-kingdom, roofed in evergreen branches, drinking rivers, antlers held proudly to the sky. When finished I asked the bear to show me where my deer-brother had gone, I asked him to point to where I could find my brother in the wooded fortress of claw scratching and crosshatched tinting. He pointed with a thick paw at a dark space in the middle of the wall, where nothing had been carved, a space left entirely open. I asked him *Is that a river or a lake?* He only exhaled a nine of diamonds and flew out through my open door.

In these woods, a bear is not for keeping.

But underneath one bear is always another, and each believes the same bear-beliefs. Each bear understands how to pretend children, how to paint with paws, how to eat honey, and how to die. I pretend living, a deer-brother caught beneath my disbelief. But I invited new bears in, and each new bear left a carving on the wall, and each new bear left a space in the carving, an opening where my brother was, and each bear asked *Brother?* but could not understand what it meant to be deathly. And each bear left. And the second house I had built, with all these trees cut down to make walls that were carved into pictures, it was only for a want of brotherhood.

Then the glaciers were pooling, and it was summer, and I lit a fire. I arranged grass and sticks in the shape of a monument in the center of this second house and I told the bears to come see my next trick. I told all of them that cards no longer bored me, that I was ready again to show them, that I was born anew. I wanted each and every bear-brother to step into that second house and feel with me the loss of an open space where living used to be. I wanted them to be bear bodies across and over and beneath one another in an agony of slow dying. I called all of the bears in, and the bears came, because bears in these woods are full of absolute belief.

In these woods, where I have come to refute death, bears and magic are to be envied.

I pulled cards from my fox-fur sleeve and held them up to the ceiling. The bears waited, quietly and with clouds in their eyes. Then I tortured fire out of rocks hammered together and smelled fire inside of fading summer skies, the feint of possibilities. I tricked the bears into believing that death was only magic. I rejected what the bears had shown me, that my brother was a gone-deer in an endless forest, a messenger bringing me death on folded paper. I rejected bear after bear by burning them all in this second house, each bear patiently waiting for new magic while its fur went alight and the room buzzed with the tinder of smoldering bears. I burned until all was ash, until there was a rawness in my belly soothed only by honey.

In these woods, where I walk out of a burning second house, where I step out of another flamed body, where I deer-seek for a new brotherly message, one to keep me living.

[the third house]

I built the third house in the center of a lake, and there was constant weeping. I made a chimney but maintaining the fire was enormous and impossible. I built gutters for the roof but the rain of lake was too much for it. I was continually pushing my chair back from the table, water filling up every pore, like being in love.

It was in this third house that I played the violin, a serenade of fins whiskering across wet wood floors. They loved it, the violin I played, swam with their gills wide, chugging landscape.

I thought that I saw my deer-brother, deep in the water, in this third house, his hooves making the sound of our childhood on the wet floor. My deer-brother the messenger. My deer-brother the endless bearer. The deer-brother that I used to run with, along a river, who asked me *How early did you know?* The deer-brother I couldn't rightly answer.

I could only answer in fish. I struck matches on their scales, but even then they would not burn. These fish, swimming in fits of brother-schools.

I thought that I saw my brother standing on the edge of this lake, standing with a note in his hand, a black dot on white paper, a message of death, but I was in disbelief. My brother looking down but I would not give in. All of my beliefs filled with fish.

So many of them, separated by such wide universes.

The third house, stacked high with lake, turned every vision into watery make-believe. I was remembering through a glass of lake, a dismissive sun, waves of fish.

I remembered my brother running next to me, us deer-brothers churning through trees. I remembered my mother with her porcupine arms, my father wrapped in leaves. I remembered a niece holding out a blanket. Then I saw my remembrances disintegrate in a watershed of failure, and all that was left was my dead body beneath everything, in the center of an endless forest.

I built this third house atop a lake so that I could sink. I built this third house in water so that I could disappear. I built this third house in a place where everything went inward because the answers are within, and I was not going to die without trying these watery remembrances.

In these woods, craved magic is a way to finish.

I thought that I saw my brother, but there was no brother to be seen. There were only thousands of fish-brothers swirling through this third house. I snatched these fish one by one in my deer-hands, tossed each up and out, to the land. These fish who were not my brothers, thrown over the lip of the water, fins flapping in pine needles while I went back to playing deadened clefs. Fish on fish on fish drying in the heat of the sun, visions glassed. Until there was only water dripping down again, remembrances of a deer-brother and a river running between us.

In these woods, it is about learning how to undrown yourself.

I remembered in watered visions, slogged steps, that I had

come here before, when I was young, had lived in these woods with my deer-brother, with our river, with a sky overhead, deer running beside one another. These were not lost woods then but bright woods, hopeful blind woods. There was so much faith in our brotherhood. We were boys running. We were deer chasing trails. There was no hiding.

I built this third house to escape. I built this third house to dissipate. I built this third house to remain hidden.

In these woods there was a deer-brother and my constant refusal to listen.

I remembered thousands of fish-dead brethren, the idea of my deer-brother on a watered edge. These forest-dreams, these lake-visions. Underneath the water I built this third house, and this third house made dreams inside of me. My third house made the world understandable in its imperfections by drawing up memories from its wellsprings, washing the brother back into me. My third house was a chimney and a roof and those full-up gutters. I played violin in that house. I sifted fish out of that house. I collapsed and drained in that house.

Those fish were all non-brothers, their scales minor chords. I can't feel gills on my neck, the opening of fins beneath my ribs. If I was a fish I would have so many brothers, and each one of them could swim in and out of me as they pleased. Every brother could be the dream I was having, and every dream could sleep in brotherhood.

Dear Brother, When did we come undone?

In these woods, I collapse and rebuild. In these woods, I do not accept death. In these woods, I see my brother, a message of dying in his hand. I hear his hooves standing still. I reject everything.

This third house was full of fish-implications: their belief in dying, my brother's deer-insistence on deathly messages, the hollow sounds of a violin underwater.

When I played for the last time, the watery walls burst. Everything that was once a house washed away. I wanted to set fire to this third house, but the lake wouldn't allow it. There was only water, dead fish on the shore. So a violin, floating mute amongst silent scales, was the best kind of fire for this house-felling, this gross fish-brotherhood bathed in fatal final music.

[the fourth house]

I built a fourth house underneath a mountain. The mountain was tall but I moved it stone by stone, tree by tree, displaced its bulk until there was a hole I could stand in. I stood in the mountain's lack and built a house there, this fourth house. I went to my axe and my saw, making planks from trees and using mud for seams. I built a chimney for the first snow, gutters for the first rain. I built shelves where the jam would go. I built cupboards for my magic tricks, for my deck of cards, for my violin and the drippings of its music. I built a corner where I could stand. I built a chair where I could sit. I built a bed to cover in a quilt of pine needles and moss. I built my mother to rock me to sleep and my father to cook breakfast in the mornings. I built a picture frame and a picture of my brother inside of it, to keep track of what was missing.

When I was a child and my brother was a child, we were deer and we ran through these woods, our hooves light with wildness, our mouths open to mountain air. My brother would dip into the river and I would follow. We would wade. My brother would raise his head to a bird going from branches. My brother would eye a rabbit disappearing around roots. My brother would hang his antlers on the sky. I would follow, always behind, my deer-brother and this forest.

In these woods now, I am only trying to survive.

These woods are the same woods that my brother and I would run through and tumble in, but without the life that was there, without the youth or living. I awoke here, on this ground, looking up at these trees and the silhouette of my deer-brother and the sky beyond. I awoke and he was above my body, haloed in sun, holding this message: *You are dying*.

In his hand was a piece of paper, on the paper a black spot. And inside of the blackness were those remembrances of how our antlers hooked, how we punched each other in our boy-deer-faces, how our legs kicked, laughing. And inside of being pummeled was us as kids, in a herd. Inside of everything, this forest and deer-brothers running.

In these woods, escape is not attached to hooves.

In this fourth house I made a doorway with no door. Instead I restacked what was left of the mountain, tree by tree, stone by stone, leaving open only a space between the mountain's skin and my heart, so that I was living inside of a cabin inside of a cave inside of a mountain inside of the dying that I was going through, that my brother was professing.

In the darkness, I played at pretend. I pretended I was the sky. I floated. I pretended I was a river. I crossed through and past myself. I pretended I was a deer, running beside my brother. I pretended I was in a house in a cave in a mountain in lost woods where I was dying. I pretended I was only sleeping. I pretended that what felt like a bed beneath my body was instead a forest floor, soft earth and hope, light as treading hooves.

In these woods, escape is only pretended.

My brother's hand was trembling when he held out death to me, that paper with such darkness in it. I wanted my brother's trembling to have been his fear of losing me, instead of only bedside scarring. I wanted the sun to come up to hundreds of bears entering this cabin in this cave in this mountain. I wanted to slit them open, each and all of them. I wanted to swim in the blackness of red tides, to paint myself in anger, to open with all of these broken notions of brotherhood I was experiencing, all of this supposed death and my own brother telling me the rules of dying. I didn't want to sleep as it was, only dark and quiet, forever.

In these woods, my knife grew meaningless.

In this fourth house, after decades, the dark proved too much. On every wall was a sky, and in all the skies there were no stars. My brother never reappeared, no other bears came, and the blood on the walls from the first bear dried and I could no longer paint words. There was no benefit to living in a house in a cave in a mountain. It did not entice the deer back into my brother, so I burned the fourth house inside of the cave, inside of the mountain.

Deer-brother, Please come toward the light.

The flames were monotonous and bright. The mountain sighed back down into itself as the structure deflated, one hollowed-out bear within, red angry words on walls, and me walking back into these woods.

In these woods, I want to undo what has been done. In these woods, there are so many houses to build and burn down. In these woods, my brother handed me a note, and the note said I was dying. In these woods, a hundred bears will never equal a deer-brother, our hooves through trees, down paths, how we first began our living.

[the fifth house]

I built a fifth house near the river. I placed my head under its water and drank. I was a deer just like my brother, as I had been when we were young with our first antlers, when we lowered our necks to drink from the river. We would run in those woods until the sun dissolved, until the river froze. Those were skies to be believed in. Those were stars held up by hopeful strings. Those were different woods than these.

In these woods, standing beside this river, I am lost. I don't know where I came from. I left a trail of yarn, what was a scarf, but when I follow it, I am only led in circles. I loop trees and rocks but don't come to any understanding. My deer-brother says that this is where I am to die, these woods of death-beginnings.

I built this fifth house of scarf yarn, layered it up into walls and windows. I worked the yarn. I built a chimney for the first snow and hung gutters for the rain. I planted flowers in the front to greet my brother when he returns, when he brings a scythe instead of a black dot on a scrap of paper. And if he never does, if I never see him again, the flowers will light like summer, my scarf yarn to flames in front of this house, and everything will burn.

I have a knife carved from the first fox's bones, and it is here, with these flowers, our next brother-moment pending.

I keep a careful eye on the trees. I wait for my deer-brother to return. I listen for his hooves. These woods will not abandon me, though I am lost, though my brother is hiding in its furs, though death has been messaged to me and I have refused it.

In these woods, there is only coming-death. There is no living.

I have skinned or burned all the animals I've encountered. The foxes, the bears, the fish. They are not my brothers, and what I am looking for might be inside of them, buried deep. The yarn-house, this fifth house, it led me in circles until I was back and within myself, unsure about everything. And the darkness there, in the last moments of being, is a torment. My comfort: the burning of these houses. When we are dying, there is no other way to exist.

In these woods is a history.

In these woods is how history opens up from inside of us.

I do not want to die.

Dear Woods, What was it that you wanted to tell me when you opened your mouth so wide? There were pine needles in there. What does it take to perform that kind of magic? I've learned that beneath those woods, where your roots are buried, is permafrost, a cold that never shrinks, and that is more frightening than your open yawn.

In these woods, my fifth house was built on the shreds of living, on what was left in my antlers.

Dear Death, I am a mountain of fear and doubt.

I spark a fire and it grows.

As deer we breathed woods, my brother and I. We ran lifetimes. Rivers are generous and a moon rises even as my fifth house burns. These flames expand and I am on a bed of yarn, beneath a roof of yarn, inside walls of yarn. Animals scatter back to their homes in the branches and hollows, afraid to watch me burn. This fifth house, this scarf-yarn house, it goes quickly to ash, my body the loneliness inside of it.

In these woods, it is about learning how to remember our deer-brotherhood. It is about building lives that we can burn in effigy. It is about understanding all we have kept hidden.

In these woods, where I am lost and alone.

Dear Brother, Remember: there are always still those young woods we ran in before the truth was out, before all this fear about difference.

[the first house /// rebuilt]

My brother is not a fox. This I why when the first fox came to see me, I trapped him in my first house and lit the walls on fire, watched him scramble up the wood in search of air. I sat in a chair next to him, his paws scratching deep, flames surging upward. I smoked a pipe and felt us burn.

There is not a brother in these woods I want to leave unskinned.

When I opened the second fox's chest, his heart was still beating. I put that heart in my pocket. It is a waste to ignore love, even if it is so far from brotherhood.

In these woods, clouds billow into bears and foxes and fish. Clouds are smoke from my burning houses. Clouds become attic space for us as we rise into the blue.

The pipe I smoked when the first fox was burning, when the second fox's fur coated my arms, was a pipe stuffed with autumn leaves. A sprig of fall smoke curling skyward.

Dear Woods, Is there ever a time when death does not?

When we were children, my brother and I, we would run through these woods. We would stoop at the river and float sticks. We would carve branches into spears and puncture each other with their points. The knife I used to open this second fox, it is the same knife that will be my last knife. Memories, built up in items, are the only kind of history I hold to.

Dear Woods, I am at a loss.

In these woods, cloud movement in the sky is an extension of our last veins. We are bleeding, brothers.

The first fox, I tricked him into my first house by calling his name. It was the name of my brother. I called to him *brother, brother* until his paws were on the doorstep. Once he was inside I latched the door, struck rocks to other rocks, and sparked up a fire that would eat our bodies. The look on that first fox's face was terror, a realization that *brother* in fox means something different than *living*.

In these woods, escape is only pretending to die.

Dear Woods,

My deer-brother had ten daughters. I watched each of them wake in his arms. I watched each of them grow pigtails. I watched each of my deer-brother's ten daughters learn to knit. His ten daughters, my dear brother. The death-blankets they hovered over me were knitted with their one-hundred brother-daughter fingers, with their twenty deer-brother-daughter hands, stories of brothers woven into the fabric.

In these woods, ten daughters from my deer-brother are in the trees, each putting her death-blanket over me. A death blanket is what keeps us warm underground when we are buried, permafrost nestling our chins. Above ground, in these lost woods, death-blankets and deer-daughters are all reminders of dying.

My first house was made of logs. I cut down the trees, used my axe. I laid trees on trees until walls were formed. I built a chimney for the first snow. I made gutters for the first rain. I built a doorstep for the first fox to cross, a house to trap him inside of, a home to burn us both down. I built a roof over our heads, to gather smoke like clouds. I built a crown from the second fox's head, to wear atop my own in a mimicry of brotherhood.

There is no brother like a deer-brother. There is no sound like what a burning fox makes.

There is, in these woods, no meaning to the word *alive*.

I awoke in these lost woods, this forest-maze, in this forest repeating itself on all sides, in this forest where there is no escape, where even if you walk far enough, as I have in my second fox's skin, fur blown by wind, crown alight in sun, there is no end.

Dear Woods, Have I mentioned the wind?

My brother is a deer. My brother is not a fox. My brother is not the skin that I wear on my skin, not the heart that has stopped beating in my pocket, not the death-blankets that my deer-brother's ten daughter-hands have knitted me, have laid me beneath.

I built a first house to get rid of the foxes. I built a first house to find my brother, but he is still deer-hiding. Deer-hiding is never coming out. Deer-hiding is delivering a message of death and then disappearing into darkness. My deer-brother's tail was only a spark of white, turning and running by the time I had raised my antlered head.

Dear Woods, When we were children, we were a river running.

I see clouds as bears, clouds as foxes, clouds as fish and smoke from burning-down houses.

In these woods, where the trees are repeating themselves, I feel the pull of a deer-brother, his magnetism from inside the treeline, though he remains hidden. He is scared of facing me again. His message was death and I have refused it, will continue disbelief, but how to talk with a brother that is dying, who refuses to believe.

Dear Brother, I cannot live forever in a burned-down house, in the skin of another fox.

Deer-brother, Come back to see me.

In these woods, hiding is never saying what you mean. In these woods, as the sun goes down, clouds make the shape of dead foxes. In these woods, my first house burns to the ground with me inside it. My belief in love is waning. There may never be a deer-brother who returns. There may never be another sky above me that is not the sky of these lost woods, that is not a lost sky, that is not a sky trying to claim my body for its own.

I see bear and fox shapes. I see fish swimming in smoke. I see a deer-brother playing at disappearance.

In these woods, there is sometimes only remembering: we were children, running.

Dear Woods, What would it hurt to wait just a little while longer?

[the fourth house /// rebuilt]

I woke with my brother standing above me, a note in his hands.
What happened was that I felt loss.

I built my fourth house in a cave in a mountain in the midst of
these lost woods. A forest filled with foxes, a forest of bears,
a forest with fish in flight. There was a river, and we could
remember it, my deer-brother and I, as we dipped our antlers
down into its pools.

When I was a child we made paper airplanes, flew them
together out into trees. We curled their wings to create lift.
We forked their tails. We found snakes nesting under boughs.
With my brother we created a brotherhood that was only the
two of us, running. Then my brother had ten daughters and I
had no love left to secret away, and there was this forest I woke
to, was told to die in.

In these woods there are branches like arms.

I did love when I was younger, but I loved a kind of love that
my brother could not parse. I spoke in a tongue that was more
fish than deer, more fox than deer, more bear than deer. I ran
back inside of our childhood forest instead of running out of it.
Or I slept when I should have woken up, or I threw away our
bones and kept only skin, became a fox when I should have
been a brother.

In these woods, love is of another kind.

I always wanted to hold ten sets of my own daughter-hands, not these brother-daughters who are lovely but not mine. I wanted to see the forest come to an end, lost woods regaining ground. Instead I built houses. Worlds inside of worlds. Instead I burned my unkempt truths.

A bear crept into this fourth house, and I was standing in the darkness with an open knife, waiting to take his guts in my fingers, to feel the warmth of living. In this fourth house, in this cave in this mountain in these woods, smearing bear-blood on black walls, a brother mine-field in front of me, I refuted death.

I am in search of my deer-brother because I want to tell him what it means to be like this. I want him to see beneath my deer-skin, down to the brother-core, where there are love-words and moments of sky unencumbered by clouds. I want my deer-brother to see his deer-brother, no matter what. Instead it was a note of dying, the death he handed me, dear brother, and these lost woods always circling, houses built and burned and built and burned.

The bear who entered this fourth house, he pretended to be my brother. He held open his chest and showed me the faux brother-heart beating there. He called to me, *brother, brother,* but there was no brother in that bear. There was only blood, mounds of blood. There was only fur and skin, only a lost painting in his veins that I scribbled on the walls of this house, this cave, this darkness.

I wanted more bears, I wanted bear after bear, I wanted to open up the world and let it spill. There was no woman in front of me, no way to have ten daughters who were mine. Instead only this lost forest, these lost woods, my brother's daughters laid over my body, the bright darkness of this fourth house buried and then burned inside a mountain.

In these woods I burn down everything I can't understand.

I built this fourth house in a cave inside a mountain. I picked out the space, rock by rock, carried in the trees, cut them to walls, stacked the walls against the cave's skin, made there a fourth house. I left the doorway open as an invitation to bears who believe they are brothers, though I only had one to spread blood-lovely on the walls of this.

In these woods, *brother* does not mean *bear*. Living is subjective.

When I set the fourth house on fire, when it burned up, there was a moment it went bright, where the cave showed itself before I burned, before the doorstep burned, before it was all dead again, and the painting beautiful there on the flaming walls.

In these woods, I don't believe in dying. My faith is in hapless bears who wander into the hearts of others. My hope is in fish, in rivers, in the ash and soot on my bare feet. I hold out for an end to lost woods, a return to living, though my deer-brother has not come back since his pronouncement of death.

In these woods, we are standing too far from one another.

In these woods, deer-brothers come undone.

In these woods, there is this brother-loss.

[the first fox]

My deer-brother had ten daughters. My ten nieces. They leave me death-blankets in the limbs of trees, knitted-webs I pass through at night when I am between houses, when I night-walk in these woods searching for my deer-brother. The sounds my nieces make in this forest are so close to wind that I cannot tell their worlds apart. It is a *Happy Birthday* chorus, a memory of living, a sound as if I was alive. My brother, his deer-daughters, they rain down nighttime tuck-ins of death, of final resting, but I won't believe I have died until there is more than these woods shivering my body.

Dear Woods, Is there ever a way to stay whole-heartedly warm?

Underneath it all, there are these woods that we walk in. I am walking in these woods. I am between houses and the first fox I killed in my first house, the house I burned down inside of my first death-dream, he is following me. That first fox is carving a line of trees between us, that fox who is not a brother. My first fox should be dead but he is not. My deer-brother says I should be dead but I am not. I refuse to accept his message, delivered to me in brother hands when these woods opened up.

In these woods, there is no shame in firing up our bones.

My brother was a deer and we were running. And us deer, we tangled antlers in our younger skins, the echoes of cracking under snowy skies, the wrestling of our brother-love. Our velvet antler-crush, our hooves on ground.

Dear Brother, Why would you ever agree to deliver me this death?

A fox is not a brother, but a fox would never ask me to die. A fox would carry my death on his shoulders, on his singed fur. A fox would let me burn down his ribcage like a tiny house, my heart inside of it. A fox is not a deer, and a brother is not a messenger of death.

In these woods, the ash is the burning.

My brother was a deer running away, back into these woods. I am the slower animal. I leapt to his trails but there was only snow on the way. My brother was maybe never meant to be the messenger but opened his brother-hand and there was a note, a black dot on a white page. It was maybe left while he was sleeping, after cradling his ten deer-daughters into their forest-dreams. So here I am, chasing behind, snow covering up our hoof-prints.

In these woods I don't believe in death. I forfeit all rights to understanding. I take no stake in this.

In these woods, I remember being a brother, running, and the woods with their river, and us as deer-brothers. I remember my ten nieces, their deer-small hands. I remember scratching our antlers on tree-bark, cutting my years. I remember what I was before the woods were lost, before I was lost in them, before my deer-brother was hiding in this treeline and I was a burning down houses.

In these woods, there are deer-hearts and death-blankets and fright.

Between the burned down houses and me, the trail I have left, there is the haunting of death. There is the notion of dying, running its hands up my deer-back. There is remembering my deer-brother's daughters, their daughter-hands, the messages we don't want to receive.

In these woods, I am in the middle of a gathering. All these hooves. I am surrounded by snow and deer, but none of them are my brother. These are only deer and my brother is not in their number. I raise my hand into the air to show them the message, the black heart underneath our white sternum, and they scatter.

In these woods, the notion of death is a gunshot winging above us.

My ten nieces were all still young deer-daughters the last time I saw them, nudging death-blankets down on me, my mouth only a buzzing gape, the words on my tongue: *I will not die.*

In these woods, I ask for what cannot be.

In these woods, there is the sound of brother on brother.

I am shrouded in deer-daughters and this inability to believe.

In these woods.

Death-blankets are how lovely daughters, in their brother-form, they lay us down to sleep. A deer softly beaten, antlers tipped groundward. My deer-nieces are unbound daughters sweeping through woods, their arms toward an endless sky, a gorgeous hum in their youth.

In these woods I am a mockery, this death I refuse to be.

In these woods, I am hemmed in sadness.

Deer, a river, brother and brother and daughters held above us.

In these woods.

My brother handed me a white note marked with a black spot. In the sunlight over my head, I see the shape of my body, curled underneath a death-blanket, giving up. Ten deer-brother daughters swinging above my ribs. Ten deer-daughters with unfurled wings. Ten brother-daughters resting me down: *Uncle, Uncle.*

Deer-Brother, You said you saw god, so I wept. You said I would be okay but I'm not. How is it that your words and my existence can be so different? How is it that these trees in this forest reveal me, from outside in, my bones and the temperature of this deer-skin? And how, dear brother, are your daughters so beautiful?

To end without beginning, that is a certain kind of fire burning down houses, in these woods.

[the sixth house]

To build the sixth house I cleared the forest. Swept away every tree, every river, every mountain. I made a plain and planted thin-rooted grasses that would never green. I hung their yellow garlands around my neck in a collar of dry stalks. I used an axe and a saw. I cleaned the lost woods from themselves. And from atop this sixth house I could see every angle, every distance, the place where the world starts to repeat, where our flat map falls outward.

In these woods that are not woods anymore, I can walk forever. It is all looping. There is no end.

In these woods that are not woods anymore, I am lost.

I can see, standing on the peak of this sixth house, planted on its roof, the sky above me and the ground-plain below. There is nothing else.

I cleared away this world to look for my brother. I awoke and he was above me, handing out a message of my dying. Then my deer-brother turned tail and ran. I heard the hooves leaving but could not follow fast enough. There was either too much snow on the ground or too much sun in my eyes. I don't want to die. I don't want to be an ending.

In these woods that are not woods anymore, there is forever

mixed with endings.

To cut down every tree is to build up the muscles that muscle our bodies, to scare every animal out into the mirrored-glass that is the end of days. The bears and foxes, the fish. With each tree falling animals ran and ran into the distance, into where I could not see them anymore, and it was as if they no longer mattered.

In these woods that are not woods anymore, I am alone.

I built the sixth house of cleared trees, each and every plank, the roof and walls and floor, trees to be lost in. I built a chimney for the first snow and gutters for the rain. I stood on its porch and looked across the deer-less plain. I stood on the roof and held my face up to a sun that was burning. I stood in its home-heart and felt the loss of a deer-brother.

I don't believe in dying.

I cleared this ground to find my brother, but no matter how I run, even in the deer-shape I am, it is too far. It is always too far in these woods that are not woods anymore. The sun raping this no-more-cover of trees. And the rains that come, when they come, will have nothing to keep them from washing away our faces.

I built gutters on this sixth house, but funneling down sadness is only burying trees into walls, is only opening the sky to full sun and never clearly seeing our deer-brothers.

Once there were bears who frequented my house, looking for magic tricks. Once there were foxes who came along, pretending brotherhood. Once there were fish who swam in and out of me like music. Once there were deer, once there was a river, once there was a brother.

In these woods that are not woods anymore, there is an overwhelming sense of loss.

What I cleared from the land for this sixth house I burned on its lawn. What trees I didn't use for the walls or the ceiling I stacked into towering effigies. What water there was in the river I set fire to with careful arms, watching the world dry. What lakes there were the land swallowed whole in its aging. What mountains there were I dug up, handful by handful, and placed under the ground in mountain-coffins, burned to keep away the smell of dying.

This sixth house, I burn alive inside it, the shade from its ceiling nothing to stop the heat of an over-opened sun.

I want to cover my body in honey, to smear these worlds across my nakedness and wait for bears. But there are no bears here, there is no devouring. They have all run, following away the mountains and trees and rivers.

In these woods that I wish were still here, there is always one begetting another. There is a birth that births. There are always new beginnings.

In these woods that I long for, are all my desires.

A plainsong is sadness. A plain in these lost woods is overwhelming.

My brother said to me *I am so sorry for this* and what was on his brother-face was brother-sadness, even though when I said, with bright sun in my eyes, *Why?* he was already out into the edge of nothingness.

In this sixth house, my body burning up, I want only these

woods back. In this sixth house, with my arms aflame, I walk outside and light the plain on fire. I burn the world in its middle, walking circles ever-outward until all is waging ash and this sixth house is wiped clean and my burning body disappears.

In these woods I have razed, I only want trees in which to wander, to search again for a deer-brother who has lost himself for having to play death.

In these woods that I seed, I only want a deer-brother who is possible. I am only looking for his deer-face, his deer-mouth.

In these woods that have started again, breeding, I am grounded. My sixth house has burned and around it is growing up again this river, a pooling lake, the woods I am lost in, that we used to run in, where the deer in me is back to being.

Deer-brothers. A lost woods. Another house burned down.

Then the bears and the foxes and the fish and the deer. It all grows back, fills in, and I awaken into a second death-dream. I wake to find my deer-brother standing above me, a note in his hands, his hooves on the ground and his deer-mouth saying, *You are dying.* And when I look up at him, deer-longing in my eyes, to ask of my dear-brother *Why?* he is lost again, and there are only woods where his deer-antlers once were.

[the first daughter]

The first daughter I had was the hardest because she was made of stone. This was a daughter I could hold and hug. This was a daughter I could not break. I wanted a daughter the opposite of fragile because I was not meant to have children. I was only meant to pretend family. I was only meant to run deer-woods and imagine what it would be like to live.

My brother and I, when we were children, we were deer, and we ran. There was a river that swung through these woods and we would follow from one side to another. We started into the trees where the river went and we ran, one alongside the other, pushing our way through, always on its shore. There were our antlers and hides, and then the other side of the forest where the river went, and we could stand in our deer-brother skin looking out at a horizon where the river scrambled.

I want to say to my brother, when I catch him, *Where did that river go?*

The sky, in these woods, it is a pale skin.

In these woods my deer-brother is missing and I am chasing him.

You are dying he told me, but I do not believe in death. There is more than this.

In these woods, we are both lost.

In these woods, a river used to mean a river.

My first daughter was a smooth-sided stone, birthed from my hands, held close to my face. I whispered to her. I taught her everything, all in one unending day, the water beside us, all the other daughter-stones in the brother-river waiting to be birthed.

Why? she would ask of me, her stone-father, but I had no answer. *Because I plucked you up* I wanted to say. *Because you are meant to be* I meant. *Because* was all I could say, and even that I spoke in absolute quiet.

My deer-brother had ten daughters, ten deer-daughters with deer-daughter smiles rising above forests. My deer-brother, his fatherhood, the soft pounding of hooves and love.

I don't know what I am doing in these woods.

In these woods, I am lost.

My stone-daughter is unbreakable, but she needs more than me to live. In these woods, my stone-daughter's rock-heart tears between her father and this river.

In these woods, where our deer-running was born.

My brother and I ran this deer-forest, beside this river, for all our youth. But this collection of trees now is a lost woods, a smattering of gone, a forever encircling of branch-arms and a river that cannot be followed to its end. When I picked this stone-daughter from the river and called her *Stone* she wept river-tears, wanting a mother not a deer-father, not what it was

I had to offer in these lost woods.

I sung my stone-daughter to sleep, beneath a pine, touching her stone-face under stone-eyes, closing them into dreams. I sung of her, my stone-daughter, about a world where the river had an end, where the horizon was not a challenge, where there was a start, a beginning, one that housed a river's mother, waiting with open loving arms.

In these woods, there are so few words for *mother*.

My brother and I, when we were deer-children, we had a mother. She baked us bread and held cookies to our deer-faces. Our mother was a stand of trees. Our mother was a lake where a river ran. Our mother was a kind of overflowing. My stone-daughter does not have a mother. Her only mother is a river, and a river is water that never stops.

For my stone-daughter, I will never be enough.

We do, underneath pale lost-woods sky, what we must.

In these woods, I remember never being in love with the woman who was in love with me, my deer-parts unable to build faux-love. My deer-brother knowing I was never going to love this woman.

In these woods, my stone-daughter is crying, making her own river, but I am only a deer and not a father, a hand covering up moonlight and not the song I want to sing. My stone-daughter awoken from her own first death-dream, the reality of stone-living.

Stone, I say, *I am so very sorry.*

In these woods, I will drown my stone-daughter, so she won't continue to feel this way.

In these woods I take her to the edge of the river, I hold her in my hands. *Shhh* I whisper, and I nudge my deer-antlers in the direction of the water.

I know what it is like to wake in these woods, to feel both familiar and uncertain. I understand the meaning of dying, but I do not believe in its trees.

In these woods I purge her stone-face under river-water, my deer-face looking on. I cry woods, I cry forest, and my brother stands at the edge of it, watching us both, my deer-self and this stone-daughter, this motherless-living, his regret at everything that was me and the way it all changed.

Until my stone-daughter rests in a posture of love, in these woods, where I am lost.

[the second house /// rebuilt]

The bear came back to defend himself. He brought his paws and a club to raise. The bear wanted to look down my sleeves. He was seeking aces. I told the bear I didn't have any sleeves, my naked body open to the sun on my front porch.

In these woods, I rebuilt this second house just to lead him in.

There are no tricks here I said to the bear, who looked like the first bear but who was the first bear's brother. *There is no magic in my hands* I told him. But he looked longingly on my nakedness. I felt ill-prepared.

I'm not sure, bear, what we are both looking for.

This second house was built on the side of a valley, over a mountain range, where a glacier was coming towards us, both the bear and myself wanting only to move on. The glacier's legs were icing down the slope, making of our valley a longer valley, in the place where I rebuilt this second house.

I don't want to believe you the bear said to me after a wait, and the glacier moved into our mouths. *That is different from disbelief* I said, *your not wanting to believe.* But the bear kept his paws up, the club steady, tempted to separate my head from its body.

Go ahead, maul me I told the bear, only because my deer-brother had already admitted my death. *What more can be done?* I asked him, though I was really only questioning my existence.

Dear brother I wanted to say, *doesn't a glacier mean anything anymore?*

This second bear was on the porch and I was in a death-dream. This second house rebuilt so I could ask him in, his paws still raised to the air, a jar of jam resting on a shelf. *Bread?* I asked, and the bear nodded. *Lemonade?* I asked, and we set about our waiting.

I built this second house on top of the ashes of its second house-brother, the house I had already built here, the house that had housed the first bear who loved my card tricks so much that he invited his bear-brothers to see my sleight of hand, the same bears who I barricaded in that second house and burned down to the haunted ground of these woods.

I burned those bears and their first-bear brother, my first-self, that second house in this valley, with its glacier. The rest is all looped moments, slow tumbling.

I built this second house out of lost woods, used their ghostly bark and tree-innards to build skyward. I built a roof to cover my head, walls to hold us in, gutters for the rain and a chimney for the first snow. And I was careful about the porch, made perfectly fit for two deer-brother hooves and two bear paws, both to stand one beside the other, when we came to question living.

I see you brought a club with you I said, and the bear wielded it higher. *That is nice* I told him, weary already of the jam and the bread and the lemonade.

The bear didn't speak because he was in my lost woods, in this second house rebuilt, and it is impossible to tell a real world of living from our pretend-shell of glaciers.

In these woods we want for so much, but only offer *More jam?*

I felt like the bear wanted to say something, wanted to speak, but instead he sat at the table I had built, in this second house, dejected. This is why I burn down the houses I build. They are all, at some point, filled with too much sorrow.

In these woods, I am lost.

In these woods, there is a bear seated at my table, and he is feasting without opening his bear-mouth.

I had a deer-brother and he had deer-hooves. In my path is both glacier and bear, so I took time reconstructing this second house, building it back up in the shape of a perfect fire, so that the bear and I would have comfort in our waiting, reassurance that when we set fire to our own skins, holding bear-hand in brother-hand, the ashes would be all that was left.

In these woods, in this sinking valley, we both know magic is pretend.

In these woods, the river will dowse our flames, even as it winds away from us.

[the first fox /// re-burned]

The first fox makes me remember the first house, which was the house I built when I arrived, when the sky and my deathly eyes opened. There were mountains and a river, the first fox walking alongside me, a pretend-brother.

In these woods I haven't seen birds in lifetimes.

These woods are a difficult place.

The first house was made of trees. I used an axe. I used a saw. This first house was the forest felled and I made walls. I made walls and a floor and a ceiling to hold above my head. I made a chimney for the snow and gutters for the rain. I gave the first house a first porch so I could stand upon it, look out from it, see the ring of lost woods surrounding me and gesture at its fox-lined interior.

When I call, the word comes out *Disbelief.*

My brother was deer-hooves, my brother was antlers. My brother was possessed with a message and the message was my dying. When I was a deer and we were a herd, we chased the river through these woods, knowing every branch and lichened rock. This was us as deer-children, eyes cocked to every pinpoint of light, ears turned toward every wind-rustled pine needle. This was our deer-ancestry, our deer-childhood.

My brother, his dear face.

In these woods, my brother has not returned. He left his message and was gone. When I looked from the note to his face, he had turned the color of sky, had disappeared and I was left to weep deer-rivers.

In these woods, there are no directions.

I stood on the porch of my first house, before it burned down, and the first fox crept into my head. He was sneaky, this fox, and though he wanted to be a brother and pretended as best he could, he was a fox, and a fox is never a brother. A fox can only want to be and fail. This is how the world starts on fire. This is how foxes burn.

That fox inside my head was the first fox, an instant of death-dreams unwound. I invited him to play catch with honey on our tongues, and we held deer-hoof in fox-paw, felt the fires rise up around us. This first house, these lost woods, the first fox and my lost deer-brother.

In these woods, our burning down is a lack of knowing.

In these woods, sometimes there are only weeping flames.

Dear Brother, When was the last time you remember us playing through this river? It was yesterday, a lifetime long, and inside of the river were our reflections, and I was unafraid. Do you remember what that was like, to be running, to be deer-brothers, antlers caught in antlers?

[the first fox /// rebuilt]

I remember the first fox when he came to me at the first house. I was on the ground, looking up into a death-dream, and he was at the precipice of these woods, hunting me.

In these woods the clearest feeling is that of living. I remember being alive. I remember it as if it were this first house, the house I built and stood in, waiting for a first fox to give up his righteous skin.

These woods are an uneven place. Mountains bow to glaciers, valleys rise to sky.

I am lost in these woods.

I built my first house out of trees. I used an axe and a saw, and the first house rose out of my heart towards the cloud-curtained sky. I built the first fox out of fur. I made and remade the first fox until he was as close to a deer-brother as I could imagine. He could never be a brother, but with lost woods haloed around his skull, there was the magic of pretending.

In this first fox was my first pretend-brother.

I open my mouth and the word *Hope* comes out.

Dear Pretend-Brother, How nice it is for you to come here, your heart in your hand.

When I was a child I was a deer and I had a deer-brother and we would run through these woods, chasing this river, watching our antlers make shadows. When I was a deer I had a brother and his sun was both our suns.

My brother says I am dying but I do not believe him.

Dear Brother, Where are you hiding?

In these woods, the only longing is to find a way out.

On the porch of my first house I stood and watched the sun set. The first fox was there, soaking up trees, his skyline a river in my head. This is a death-dream, and a lost woods, and I am waiting for instructions. Sometimes there is only failure. Sometimes we cannot remember being deer-brothers, facing outward, awaiting word of whatever will happen next.

I remember fire. I remember how it felt to be flaming.

My first fox was the knowledge of burning down, inside myself, and how we can't escape. The ashes giving way to more foxes, to more houses, and there are only so many words to scream from our deer-mouths. We do not rise up. We cave and reappear. We flame, this first fox holding my deer-hand, us burning down together.

In these woods, tears are a symbol of want.

Dear Brother, Do you remember what it was like to have a brother? I was smaller than you and our antlers were different shapes, but when we ran this river, it always gave way to more river, and we were smiling.

[the second fox]

There was a second fox. And the second fox was more a brother than the first, but only because he stood taller and wanted less of me. The second fox was in these trees for shade, on my porch for sunlight. The second fox came outward from the forest, where my ribs still hang, holding in his jaws the power of a treeline.

In these woods I do not believe in death, no matter the brother who brings it to me.

In these woods, foxes mean so much more than dying.

I built a first house, I made a second fox, I walked through doorways.

I covered myself in honey and lay down in a meadow. I waited for the bears to devour me, but there was only the second fox hovering nearby, ready to lick my wounds.

In these woods, I need help remembering what a brother is.

I built the first house from trees. I used an axe and a saw. I used my hands. I uprooted the forest and made it in the shape of walls, in the posture of a roof, in the open palms of floorboards where I could stand, looking out on this death-dream.

I said to the second fox *Where is your fox-brother?* but he only moved to the shadows.

In these woods is where I learned that not all foxes are brothers.

My brother was a deer, the same deer-brother who messaged my death then fled.

In these woods, death is a dream, and deer-brothers always vanish.

In this first house I made sunlight and placed it on a shelf. The sunlight glimmered. I wanted to forage my brother's return, but he never came. I trapped the first fox in that first house and burned the both of us down, flames galloping over our limbs, my deer-brother staying gone. So when the second fox came, I took his hide for my skin, wrestled the fur from his body and wore it as a cape, became a king of lost woods, made his skull my cavernous crown, carved knives from his bones. This is how I attempted to negotiate my brother's return.

In these woods, there is no returning.

I open my mouth and the word *Scepter* falls out.

Royalty still means lost.

In the first house I did not save room for hope, or I did not understand how to build it, so I went without and the foxes went altogether, and the three of us, we burned and shed and caved, death-dreams taking over.

In these woods there are foxes and deer. Bears. Fish. In these woods there is a notion of dying. In these woods, all of this is fear.

The second fox was a blessing, his skin ripe. The second fox was almost a deer-brother, but instead I draped his fur about my shoulders and felt the wind as he must have felt it, this second fox without a first fox brother, and my own deer-self without a deer-brother hand to hold.

In these woods, I am failing in my disbelief.

Dear Brother, Do you even remember me?

[the first non-death-dream]

To fall asleep I hold one hand in the other and pretend as if one of those hands is not mine but someone's who cared enough to hold me. Down deep, longing is shaped like birds in trees.

In these woods, I wake to dreams.

I had a brother. I was a deer. These are the moments holding me together.

In these woods it is death-dreams and sunlight, the two moaning inside each other. But then there was this first non-death-dream, where the world was icebergs, where I was crushed on all sides by penguins, where being a deer meant nothing.

There was ice, and my hooves were slipping.

Waking from anywhere to here is bruising.

In this dream that was not a death-dream, the cold was frostbite on my elbows and I couldn't feel any hands touching my hands. I was only a person and not a deer-brother and the penguins were all the small feelings I'd ever had or wanted to have.

In these woods, where dreams turn forests to ice, so cold in their unearthing.

I shiver and wake and comb through the pieces.

This is how I dream *hope* and *love* and *stability*. This is how I remember that this death-dream is inescapable, that my once-living was shaped from within, from truth, that all the small feelings rendered on an iceberg in black and white are meant as something greater.

A penguin is not a word or a cloud. A penguin is an iceberg-moment. And a huddle of penguins is a mass of sorrows, and this kind of non-death-dream would be better served as a warm sun above a house built from trees, lit by a timber-heart. And when I wake again it isn't waking at all, which is how my brother meant to say it.

[the second non-death-dream]

When I woke to the second non-death-dream, I was on a beach where the water was receding and there were white-caps, antlers beneath the water. There was both beach and ocean. There was sky.

The water blue-green and the sky white clouds, I dreamt lilac bushes, green and purple bordering the sand, where the shore meets the open expanse of plains beyond.

In these woods, where we are color-flooded.

Waking to a dream that is not a dream is what it means to be between you and the you that used to be. My death-dream is of houses and burning, of foxes and bears and fish. My death-dream is a brother delivering a message of dying and then his disappearance. My death-dream is about trying to find him again, seeking truth. My death-dream is about searching for a brother where a brother is not. But these non-death-dreams, they are about deciding what it means to be awake.

In these woods, in this non-death-dream, where does an ocean lead except to another shore, a different place just as quietly raucous?

The lilac scents drift and I stand, awaiting wakening. There is a tide. There are waves. My head swells, nears bursting, then recedes.

In these woods there is a deer standing body-deep in an ocean, in waves, in a non-death-dream. In these woods, in a dream where I am not dying, where a herd lives. The lilacs, the saltwater, the difference between what is and isn't.

[the third non-death-dream]

A bird dropped down from a branch and clutched my chest, leaving there the double-talon marks of bird-feet. I was running without wings, I was a deer, I was the shape I am when there is the most to fear. A slight moon in darkened woods.

As a herd, we have choices to make. We can choose to believe. We can choose to pretend. We can choose to hunker down beneath these woods, to make ourselves a home out of soil, to mud up a roof and tie together a stick-door. And when the world comes we can answer their calling at our door or we can follow the river up and out, secreting away, even if the river goes only on to infinite dusky horizons.

We thought we heard the rain, us deer-brothers, through the trees and their pine-needles. We thought we heard rain but it was the ground quivering beneath us, it was the shake and moan of growing up, it was how time changes us. If we were deer who watched the world patiently, we would have understood that our mother would die, that our father would die, that everything is temporary, that nothing holds forever. But we were only boys moving lividly on deer-feet, a fur-herd, listening for what we thought was rain instead of how it all burns down. So when our mother called, when our father brayed, we only looked up, raising our antlers to the sky. We only knew how to be children.

I lost my brother. He was in these woods long enough to tell me I was dying. He handed me death on paper, a black dot in white space, an unbroken blackness that meant *You are not real.* Then my deer-brother vanished. It was not magic but running away. I know he is here because I can still smell his hide, hear his hiding, I can still feel the deer-brotherhood that surrounds us.

When we were deer we spent summers searching for a baby river. We spent summers looking for the perfect dousing-rod. We spent summers pulling up every rock in these woods, seeking the world's smallest kite. We were obsessed with searching. And while we ran, the deer in us brothers, our mother and father drifted, all our lives went on, and we grew. Before long we had antlers and hooves of our own, and the movements of our parents were slower, until the brothers were all that was left. Then we searched for white in our beards, for creaking plates in our bodies. We searched for memories to hold us down, remembrances to be used as paperweights for our thinning herd.

When I sleep I dream of running in woods, a bird flying down from above, a bird I cannot outrun. A bird that dives into my chest, leaving scars on my heart.

In these woods I will not give up. I will not die in this purgatory.

My brother found daughters, ten of them. I found none. My brother found a wife and made with her these angels who throw death-blankets down from branches. My brother can still run, and I am only held here in my antlers, hoping for his return. He was a good deer-brother, and he found what he wanted, though inside I know we are both of us still only deer-children in a forest, making the choice between magic and living, between different kinds of love.

Even without my brother, even without his shadow looking deer-down on me, I search for the meaning to these dreams, to this dying. They are about the cold of death, about being underground, about trying to run away when all the shores are identical. These dreams are about brother-loss, about regret, about longing to live. These dreams are about containment, and about a lack of walls.

In these woods, I am a deer-detective.

On a tree in these lost woods was a note pinned to bark, a message saying *The trick is to remember your own name.*

I am searching for my brother. I am searching for my deer-self. That is all the clarity I have.

Dear Brother, Where is it we have gone? I watch the sun, but what of it? There are no words there.

We have choices to make. We can choose to live in a way that suits the river, the trees, our deer-brothers. Or we can choose to live as we might, building and burning down houses in an attempt to raise our brothers from the dead. We can choose to open foxes, to play the violin for fish, to entice bears with honey-covered bodies, to hold out our chests to the dreams of birds descending. We choose how we are lost.

Deer-brother, I am sorry that your ten daughters are not mine.

Deer-brother, I am sorry that your wife is not mine.

Deer-brother, My open hand is yours.

The hope is that when I find my brother, he will be standing, antlers to the sky, neck strong and upward, ready to see me again. And I hope he will take this message of death from off my back, the black spot. I hope he will crush it beneath his hooves, stamp it into the forest floor, trample my dying down into the dirt. My hope, if there is hope, is that we can one day be deer-brothers again, children loving and alive, forever running in young woods, chasing a river, shrouded in the lightness of never-ending.

As deer-brothers, we thought we heard rain, and there was rain, and the rain collected into the river, and the river ran, and the sun was bright, and we were living.

[the second daughter]

The second daughter was made of mountains, born between a valley and a glacier, where snow and ice hold up. The second daughter with hair of spun-sun, pine tree shoulders. Collar bones I watched fill with water, camped at her edge, waiting for fish to evolve. This second daughter plaguing me as much as any death-dream, this second daughter a real imagining of these lost woods, where I cannot escape. A second daughter in purgatory. A second daughter looming over a dying I don't believe in.

My brother had ten daughters, ten beautiful girls handing down death-blankets from branches, their attempt to keep the dead warm. My deer-brother and his ten daughters, each one of them with a name and a face, each of them with ten daughter-fingers on two daughter-hands, each of them forest-glowing. Daughters are what we have when we find love. Daughters are what happens when we are not lost in woods but found, holding our wives close, wandering lovely through sunlight.

Underneath the bark of trees there are remembrances.

In these woods, I stand, waiting for my second daughter to bear through the trees.

I remember: We were setting the table for a dinner with friends and the friends all had name cards that told them where to sit and the friends were with us to celebrate our engagement, this woman and my deer-self, and the friends had all brought bottles of wine and flowers. The friends with handshakes and hugs and teeth wrapped in smiling. And my deer-brother was amongst them, and the carving knife on the wooden table, and the clean plates, and a roasted bird.

I remember: There was a toast where someone said everything about it all. There were glasses clinked together and there were no foxes at the table, there were no bears seeking honey. These were friends as dinner-guests and we were in a valley of dreaming, where the ground was soft and everyone went barefoot to better soak the sun.

I remember: There was pretending and I was good at it, but the stakes were too high and there seemed so much to take on. There were not bears or foxes or fish and the only one bird was not clutching my chest but roasted-dead. I was lost in wrong trees and I broke. I remember that I broke. And pretending does not allow for breakage.

I remember: There was yelling, screaming, and the friends all wafted away, and it was just a woman and a man and the man was me and the woman was a woman who loved me but who I couldn't love back. This is what it is like to be a deer in a world of women, where there is only ever the want of love and longing to run. And I only wanted to chase the river to its forever horizon. I only wanted to see what it felt like to run the world around. I only wanted to see layer upon layer of woods, woods going on into forever, the woods we ran as deer-children, so I'd never have to stop for pretending.

In these woods, I am a hobbling-deer.

In these woods, a woman was not what I wanted.

Dear Brother, Did you see the way she looked at me that night? She wanted what wasn't. So how could your ten daughters ever be my ten daughters? How could your love ever be my love? And how can I, deer-brother that I am, ever learn to be a river?

I tried to love this woman back. I handed her my heart from my deer-chest, and there it lay in her hands, a pretend river running down the middle of us. This woman who was more bird than fox or fish or bear. This woman who was not a deer. This woman who was not a brother. This brother who was a brother telling me to love: *love*. This woman I didn't love and who I couldn't give ten daughters to. This deer I was and am.

In these woods, where I pretend a second daughter who is born a mountain and raised between glaciers, the cold of my deer-hooves holding tight to living dreams.

I tried to love, but in these woods, I am only one deer without a brother. I am a deer without a river, or a deer who cannot stop following a river, or a river that cannot stop running. I am lost.

I remember: She wanted to love me, but I was impossible to love.

I remember: I was a deer wanting not what women held in their woman-bodies.

I remember: The sun moves no matter what happens in our deer-brother forests.

The second daughter was impassible because she was a mountain, because she was only alive in my pretending, and my pretending was in a forest where I was lost, searching for a deer-brother who I couldn't find, inside of a death-dream I didn't believe in. This made my second daughter implausible. This gave my second daughter, the second daughter I only imagined, the brightest sun-hair I could hope for.

I called to her *Mountain*. I called to her *Daughter*.

She was as good as a glacier in pretending I existed, that I was alive too.

In these woods there is a second daughter and a lost herd and the remembrances of a woman I couldn't love.

Mountain I said, *even the biggest moments in this world can shudder down into nothing*. I said it loudly into the valley of her heart, but she already knew. I wasn't teaching her. I was only reminding myself.

My brother is a deer in these woods. My brother rode up on hooves and handed me a message. The message was a black dot on white paper. The message said I was dying, that I was dead, but I refuse to believe. I said to my deer-brother *I refuse* but he was already deep into those woods where I have been chasing him, where I have gone to build and burn houses, where I skin open foxes looking for his deer-brother hiding, hoping for a moment of redemption, or a truth that isn't.

I remember: There was a dinner, and we were playing a game called engagement, and I was lost.

My brother wore ten daughters around him like a cloak, a robe of life. He did this deer-magic by finding a woman to love and laying with her near the river, by evolving out of these woods, making a bed of pine and wearing a halo of bees.

In these woods, I am lost.

In these woods, the world is a death-dream that only always replays.

In these woods, I cannot live or die.

In these woods, I refuse to give in to pretending.

Imagine a deer-brother loving a woman and having with her ten deer-daughters. This is pretend. This is magic I cannot fit into my sleeves. Imagine what it would be like to die every day, or to live in a day that never ends, or to be a brother without a dear friend to occupy the space between living and dreams. Imagine what this second daughter would say if she existed.

Mountain I called to her, but she was already sunken back into the ground. *Mountain?* I asked the air, the explosion of my voice rattling through glaciers and valleys, mountains that aren't my second daughter, that are only purgatorial landscape.

Dear Mountain, I would have laid you down to rest with my own hands, if you'd have waited for me.

In these woods, rivers don't wait.

Mountain, I said, *Goodbye,* though I knew she had only ever been another way of escape.

[the second house /// re-burned]

The first bear brought with him art. When we tired of tricks, the two of us, we repositioned ourselves inside of everything else and he went to work painting scratches on the walls with his bear paws, clawing at this second house, and I sat in a chair with my antlers hanging down.

In these woods, I am a deer on the side of a mountain where a glacier is slowly sliding.

In these woods, there is always the tendency towards melting.

Dear Brother, Do you remember us when we were looking in opposite directions?

In these woods I was a running river, my deer-brother beside me, young and wild.

The bear pushes his claws into my wall, draws a sprawling forest-city with a deer-brother hidden in its contours, and I can only find the antlers he has shed. There is a house around us, and I will burn it down, the two of us staring into one another as our bodies slough into flame.

These woods are a pretend forest and I am looking for a deer-brother.

In these woods, where I refute death.

Bears are not deer-brothers. Bears have only other bears, bear-brothers. And this bear calls his brethren into my second house to see the tricks I perform, sunset hovering above this cabin's roof.

Brothers, he calls, and bears drip through the doorway.

In these woods, I can only surround myself with loss.

If I am dying, then I want a bear's claws nestled near me in the dark.

I am lost in these woods, and the woods are pushing out around me. This is a woods without end. I have run the length of the trees and they are continual, the river always leading me back towards the forest's center, my deer-brother always missing. Until I am back at the second house, the first bear inside of it, his claws done with art, his bear-eyes waiting for the trickery of flames.

I built this second house to show my brother where I am, to hear his hooves scuttling on the doorstep, the clack of his deer-knees next to my own.

Deer-brother, You will never understand what dying alone is like.

I built this second house for a second time. I made gutters for the rain, a chimney for the snow. I made an open door to stand and watch the ever-growing woods. I made a roof to throw the sun off my deer-back. I took honey from the shelves and smeared it across my brother-chest, lay down in the fields where bears were already standing. I closed my eyes to the imagining of their teeth. But the bears wanted tricks, wanted to send smoke up the chimney when the snow came, wanted to listen to the sounds of spillage down gutters when the rain came. The bears had no jaws for me, for this deer-body.

I lay in these woods, covered in honey and longing, waiting. I hid in my hide. I pulled my hooves slowly across these grassy fields. I dreamt this death-dream. I dreamt of woods and of being lost in them. I dreamt of my deer-brother handing me a death-message. I dreamt of bears and foxes and fish. I dreamt of my childhood herd, of antlers.

The glacier above us is coming down, and the bears can only clamor for tricks.

Gather round I say to them, the first bear's wall-drawing behind me, a deer-brother hidden within, all of the other bears clinging to this second house and their own bear-skins.

My brother handed me a black spot on white paper, and then he vanished. I was left then, a deer-brother holding a death-sentence, holding to bears and houses, trying to burn up everything that is sacred. I was left to sift through lost woods, to find in bears and foxes and fish the one deer that is still my brother, the deer-brother who can help me understand how I am dying.

In these woods, the houses are markers, the river running. In these woods, I am stumbling.

I loved women as much as I could love women, but it wasn't enough. It wasn't enough to make ten daughters as my deer-brother had, as my dear brother spent his time doing. From a beautiful woman, ten beautiful daughters, their deer-fingers and toes wiggling. I could only be their deer-uncle, antlers at the doorstep, gifts of fish-scale jewelry and bird-hopelessness.

Dear Uncle-Brother, Where are all the women in your life?

In these woods, even my brother's ten beautiful deer-daughters see how much I've lost.

The first bear, with his scratch-drawings on the wall of my second house, he was a sign of longing, a symbol of wanting. He gathered his bear brothers in to see my tricks, because he knew the magic was burning, and he wanted flames. My first bear in this second house could never be a brother, but he could be a saint. He could look at me with his bear-eyes across the second house floor and we could make a pretend forest between us, we could scramble up an imagined mountainside, live in a glacier marriage. Then the floor caught fire, and the walls and the ceiling, all the bear brothers trampling atop one another. This second house burning with bears trapped inside, the deer-brother I was, burning down my second house made from lost-forest trees, raising smoke and blight beneath a glacier-thick sky.

Dear Woods, Thank you for all the trees.

When I yawn, second house and bear ash exhale over my deer-tongue.

There is more to bears and houses than death. There is more to belief than dying. There is more to love than what love is or has been.

[the second fox /// re-skinned]

It was a black dot on white paper. This was the message my brother delivered. This was when I woke. I was on the ground. I was looking up. I was limbs sprawled and the sky was blue fed through white. My deer-brother's shadow a star's silhouette.

The black spot stretched and raised itself in the dark block of a miniature fox waking, jaws wide in their tiny state. And the fox sat, front paws extending his fox-body upward, soaking sun.

When we were children, we ran beside this river. We ran through these trees. When we were children and the world was herds, we were deer-brothers and the sun was coming through pines. This same forest. These same trees, this same sun.

In these lost woods, I am dying.

This death-dream, this is what it is like to die. This is how it is to be lost in what seems familiar.

My brother handed me a fox-spot on sky-white paper then disappeared. I called for him but only sun pushed from my mouth. I moved on shaky hooves. I stood. I ran. The river moaned. The sun was shining and there was heat in the meadows. My deer-brother was quick and I was alone and even the tiny fox had curled back into a single black spot, nose buried in hide, ears flat to the noise of my dying.

This is a death-dream and what it means to be a deer alone in a herd.

My brother ran with me in his hind-sight. My brother looked deer-ripe over his shoulder at my hooves running. My brother and I carved a path by the river in these woods, the forest like skin. Our sun coming in pulses, through branches. Our deer-hearts overgrown with antlers.

My brother dealt me a death I cannot believe in. My deer-heart closes in the burning heat of open fields, the spaces I clear to build a first house, a chimney for the snow, gutters for the rain. I build with trees. I cut with an axe and a saw. I make windows facing these woods, from the heart inside of them, to feel the tremors of rushing woods that come and come.

The first fox burned. I skinned the second fox. Neither was my brother. My brother is still missing. My brother handed me a death-note and scuttled back to the woods. I chased him, screaming deer-bleats, but the second fox's skin only emptied scepters from my mouth. There is no amount of fox-kingship that accounts for brother-loss.

In these woods, I am an empty king.

Dear Brother, Where are you running?

The first fox wanted to slink into my house, to crawl into bed, underneath my feet, to burrow into my deer-heart as brother-lust. The second fox stood in my doorway, the first fox's ashes still smoldering, and offered up his auburn back. I cut and cut. I wore that second fox's skin as a cape, as a royal garment, as a deer-brother would in lost woods like these, when there seems no other way.

There is more to be being a fox than being a lost deer-brother. There is more to being a deer than burning down foxes. There is more to wearing skins than dragging roofs over our heads.

I wore the second fox's skin and ran through these woods. The river was constant and the forest never went weak. The pines stayed tall, the sun shining. And when the moon rose it was swollen with mockery. This second fox skinned will not suffice for love.

In these woods, I couldn't love the way we are asked to.

I am a deer and my brother is bounding through these woods. I cannot run fast enough.

In these woods I want to believe that my deer-brother's message is only a dream. I want to believe only in death-dreams. I want to believe these woods are not a purgatory between living and dying. I want to remember running beside him, our hooves pounding, wind swaying pine-boughs.

Dear Woods, Thank you for offering up this moon.

Dear Second Fox, Thank you for your skin.

Dear Wife-That-Was-Never, I am sorry that I didn't understand myself.

In these woods, the difference between wanting to love and loving is the difference between deer hooves on the ground and a fox brood in the sun. If a river stops then there is no point in running. I built a first house so my brother could find his way back. I burned the first fox so these woods would stop pretending to be a brother. I skinned the second fox because that fur, running the length of his throat, looked like an escape.

In these woods, there is no stopping.

I woke in a death-dream and it was the second fox's skin. The woods were sun and the moon was pregnant with pretending. The crying out was brother-loss.

I wanted to love. I wanted deer-daughters clamoring around my ankles. I wanted deer-drinks of river-water in moonlight. I wanted only a thin sheen of love in a forest-world where death-dreams are always close. I was not looking for a message from a brother's hand, his antlers outlined in sky.

In these woods, there is more to wanting than being wanted.

I love you the second fox said before I skinned him. *Burn him* the first fox whispered. *Please* I called to my deer-brother, though he was already missing. I dreamt of holding a deer-brother, cut out of the sky, antlers stenciled in sun, and the lost woods exhaled, and their sigh was a river, my hooves running beside it.

In these woods, I am lost.

In these woods, these are only half-truths.

Deer-brother, I will keep on in this chase.

[the seventh house]

I built the seventh house in the crook of a cloud, where it was moving upward in columns, rearing to the shape of thunder that never came. I looked at the sky from within the clouds and there was a home I could build. I made the walls from trees. I used an axe and a saw. I sank a doorway and four walls into its white, made a chimney for the snow, gutters for the rain. This seventh house as a seventh place I could burn down, if the losses became too much.

From above, in the clouds, I looked down on the forest and saw how they expanded and grew without an end-line ever showing, trees into infinity. These lost woods are the only place left. This is where I am, the deer-left part of me, hiding in hiding.

In these lost woods, we can only grow up.

Deer-Brother, I've been looking for you.

In these woods, I am more lost than I have ever been.

My brother and I were deer and when we ran together we were a herd and the herd was near a river and the river was running. We were running. When we were deer we made the noise deer make, which is only ever the hoof-step of running in forest-dirt. The sounds of forgetting. When I was deer-young

I looked up to my brother, and my deer-brother looked back at me. That brother has vanished. That brother is a deer in a woods that will never stop treeing.

In these woods, this seventh house was my attempt to live inside of a dream.

In these woods, there are only death-dreams.

A death-dream is not a dream. A death-dream is a calling. A death-dream is a command. This is purgatory, these lost woods. This is what it feels like to live while dying. This is what it feels like to burn. This is what it feels like to have had a brother and to have been a deer and then to wake in a lost woods, a black dot on white paper handed out from a dear brother who disappears into the landscape.

Sky and dreams are made from the same irreverence.

When I built this seventh house up in the clouds the walls came crashing back down through that whispering haze-lake of a sky, and I understood that creating anything in clouds was a failure.

In these woods, where my brother is hidden.

Dear Brother, I'm sad. Do you remember when we were a herd? That was a music I could listen to forever.

I built the seventh house with a chimney for the first snow and a gutter for the first rain and two chairs to sit in, for myself and my deer-brother, for when we are together again. And that seventh house, when it pulled down to the ground, the weight of wooden walls in clouds, it shattered into so many pieces that it was unrecognizable, even as a dream.

I built the seventh house without imagining how I would burn it down, up in the sky, with only a pretend sun hung above these lost woods. My deer-brother hiding away in the shadows below, always escaping my search from this seventh house, the walls that stayed for only a moment.

Deer-Brother, I am so tired.

In these woods I have been handed death, and I have refused. But the woods are never-ending and the houses I build all burn down or sink. My hooves are exhausted. And the moon never rises in the way that a moon should. I write letters to the outside but they are only in my head. I try to clarify what I've done but can't. I look for my deer-brother in his deer-hiding but I can't find him. There are bears and foxes and fish. There are deer. And in this seventh house, for a second, there are birds, all the birds the lost woods hold. They fly by, streaking, the clouds no place for pause. Dreams are not suitable for building houses in.

Dear Brother, I tried.

The two chairs I built in the seventh house crashed down with its walls and ceiling, broke the same as any other point of love. There is no spirit here. On the ground these broken chairs and my deer-sad hooves, they are quiet, lost forever beneath a cloud-world. I am stuck in death-dreams where deer no longer matter, where chairs are irrelevant, where houses don't burn down but fall straight through our wishes, caving into splinters on the solid soil-fists below.

Try clouds, try sky. Try looking up with these antlers on our heads.

My brother was a deer and our childhood was a running river and the seventh house I built in the clouds was a house to fall from the sky. Clouds are not meant for dreams, and those two chairs remain empty. I call for him, for my deer-brother, search for his hoof-sounds through lost-woods branches, but dying is a singularity, and my deer-brother has disappeared into its veins.

Try hoping. Try death-dreams.

With the seventh house broken around me I had nothing left to burn. Until a bird, landed on the ground nearby, hopped in quick flits towards my hand. Until I was holding a bird in my deer-brother hand, pinning its wings to its body, touching flame to its feathers. Until a bird was flying up towards the sky, its wings alight, its beak a burning compass.

In these woods, I refuse to die.

In these woods, where even clouds are not sacred.

[the third daughter]

The third daughter was a daughter made of sun so bright I couldn't hold her. She sprung from my eyes as I looked through a saddle of mountains. There was skyline past the crags, and my third daughter rose between them, liquid sun burning.

I woke in these woods, and my ten deer-nieces were swarming in the trees, dropping death-blankets with their milk-white arms, branches holding up their humming bodies.

In these woods, what felt like a halo of bees.

In these woods there is so much language we can't use.

This deer-brother, antlers silhouetting my face, he handed me a black dot on white paper, the moment of death. I looked into the spot on the page and my brother vanished, his deer-hooves into the trees, past where I could exist.

I have built seven houses here, and none of them remain. These lost woods are a purgatory where I pine in sun.

My third daughter, on the night her pretend-voice said *I love you*, I had nothing to give back. I did not love her, could not, because she was not real, she was not a deer-daughter but a figment, and the sun broke across her face as she waited for my response. There is love for the moon and love for the sun, but we cannot have both at once.

Dear Brother, Can you imagine how fast I sank in secret living?

In these woods, remembering a woman who once loved me.

We had dinner beneath a waterfall. We held hands. Later there was a bed and so many attempts to hump and chatter our bodies against one another. The night crushed with sun-fever looming, when she said *I love you*, and I could not say anything back.

Dear Woods, Was there ever a time when you were without trees?

A river cuts through this forest. I have followed it until I can run no farther, and it is all the same woods. There is no end. The stretch in front of me, through branches, it never closes. My third daughter, there in the sky, always exactly that sun-far away. And in the opposite direction, where the river blooms, it is the moon. And the river never ends, never truncates in a lake or in stillness, and the moon is only a reflection of what we do not have.

In these woods I want to raise a kite, buzzing towards the sky, towards a sun-daughter who never was. I want to close my eyes against the heat and feel a taut line floating in my hands.

In these woods, I imagine the impossible, which is how we survive.

I am supposed to be dying, but I refuse. I refuse to let my deer-brother dictate my death. I refuse to listen to this third daughter who only ever says *I love you*, who only shines through me. I am caught in a death-dream, and there is no running out of these woods.

Deer-Moon, Can you imagine what it would be like if you had your own lighthouse heart?

My brother is a deer and we were a herd. He is nearby, breathing. I can smell his hide. I can feel the black cold of his eyes on my deer-body. We were brothers running a river, but my brother and I, when we were deer-children, the river ran into an open field, disappeared into musk-sunsets and a meadow's song. We stood and looked. We ran until that river emptied out and we stood and watched the sun go down, a moon coming up over our shoulders. This river my brother and I chased each other down, that river of oblivion, it carried our hooves like air.

In these woods, there is no unknowing what a death-dream is.

I know: I will never love a woman. A woman will only love me once, long enough to see how wrong she is. I will never have daughters. My brother has ten of them, daughters deer-shaped, like us both, loving hearts as large and gracious as the sun. But I lived in secrets, and there are no daughters in the darkness of denial or hiding.

Because a river has two open ends, it cannot escape. A river only runs. When we were deer we ran. Now I am chasing my deer-brother, invested in his disappearance. Only he can take the message of death back from inside my head, lighten my antlers with once-again living.

In these woods, I am only one of so many animals, all of us confused and wanting, all of us searching.

In these woods, there is no finding what we have lost.

My third daughter, with her beaming hair, she floated above

me as I ran in these woods, stumbling through the ashes of seven houses built and burned, of the slaughtered foxes and opened bears, through the fish and the broken violins, the birds dropping through clouds or rising in flames. This is no magic trick. I am lost, and there is only running left.

Dear Death, How fast do we have to run, the two of us together?

My third daughter melts glaciers. I hear the swell of baking ice. This world is coming down in slow-suffocation. That third daughter, a sun, I reach to her, a deer-arm to a pretend-daughter. *Sunshine* I call.

In these woods, there is only an echo left to hear me call.

Dear Brother, I am more lost than I've ever been.

In these woods, a third daughter pretended up out of nothing, risen skyward, burning.

In these woods I am death-dreaming, deer-nieces raining death-blankets atop my body, attempting to scare away the permafrost, the ground yawning open.

I am a deer, and I am running. There is no end to these woods. I will only stop to build houses and burn them down, to protest what death is. I will only stoop to entice the animals in, the foxes and bears, the birds and fish. I will only bring the animals in to kill them, to search on their insides for the deer-brother I am missing, because I don't want to die.

Sunshine I beg, but the glacier slips, and the sun sets, and the moon is as hollow as a pretend-daughter's face.

In these woods, begging is mute. Antlers do not make sound.

In these woods, the sun weighs as much as our shoulders, and a burden is a burden.

Dear Dear, I am so sorry I could not love you. Our daughter would have been beautiful.

[the third house /// rebuilt]

I rebuilt the third house at the bottom of a lake. This lake is not attached to a river. This lake appeared in the middle of these lost woods without rain or running water. This lake is a well that burst. This lake is how we would drown our deer-selves if there was still any need to die.

In these woods, I have already been told of my death.

The first time I built this third house I built it on the water's surface and it sank faster than I could finish. I made hurried walls. I lashed a flawed roof to its head. I built a chimney for the snow, gutters for the rain. I cut trees with an axe and a saw. I hauled them into the water. I floated them into the shape of a house. I wanted to live a deer-life inside of a lake, but the water came hard, crushing the roof to the floor and flooding the gutters. I wanted to invent a living that wasn't purgatory. I wanted deer-absolution.

In the third house, sinking down, fish swam into my heart and sank with it.

In these woods, the heart is a gauge.

When I returned, after the fourth and fifth and sixth and seventh houses, after the bears and the foxes and the birds, I sought the bottom of the lake, where no rivers run, and rebuilt the third house there piece by piece. I used parts of the old walls and the former roof. There is meaning in sentimentality, no matter the maze we are in. I made a chimney for the snow and gutters for the rain. The windows wept fish and my deer-heart was satisfied, until the third house began to float, and I was faced again with failure. It breached the surface, this third house rebuilt, and I was left a deer-brother, on the stoop of a water-logged porch, listening to the vibrato of fins rising beneath my skin.

In these woods, a floating house is evidence of our collapse.

I am taunted by fish who brush my lips and whisper *Brother*. Fish are not deer. Fish cannot be brothers. Fish are the strings to a violin I play underwater, in this third house, when I still long for life, when I pretend I'm not dead or dying, when I have nothing left but to re-imagine myself in a woods that aren't lost, with a river-running brother, his deer-hooves beside me, life soaking back into us.

Every house I build is an attempt to condense the world into four walls, a chimney and gutters, an occasional porch.

They called *Brother* until finally I gave myself over, opened my mouth and let them swim in. I know they are not brothers, but they fill up the hollow parts of me. And when the third house rebuilt began floating towards the surface, me floating with it, the fish inside of me rose without choice, and there was a feeling of being found.

In these woods, I can build imaginary fish into pretend-brothers.

In these woods, the difference between failure and insurmountable waters is measured in scales.

The third house rebuilt, floating on the lake's surface, it was easy enough to re-sink. I only needed to take a breath of forest air and the whole structure, the walls and its ceiling, the floor under my soaked feet, the fish in my heart and the windows wet with loss, it all started back down, splashing and rumbling into a lake deeper than seems possible, in water cold despite forever-sun. This house is a house I cannot burn down because I am still lost, still dying, and there is no spirit of burning left to keep me afloat.

[the first non-death-dream /// re-dreamt]

A death-dream is what I wake to. In these woods, where I am searching for my deer-brother, where I refuse death, this purgatory. I've opened foxes, worn their skin as my skin. I've bled bears. I've built houses in the sky where birds drifted and fell and I've set fire to them, watched them rise in flaming feathers. I've built houses that sank upward with fish. But none of this replaces my deer-gone brother.

In these woods, nothing is simple.

Between death-dreams I have non-death-dreams. The first non-death-dream I had was of waking in tundra, my lips blued. There was ice and penguins. I was shaking. From this non-death-dream I woke half-buried in the ground of these lost woods, a patch of birds chattering in the branches above me, the mocking ghost-outlines of my brother's deer-daughters knitting their death-blankets with pale hands, the cold of dying.

In the first non-death-dream my veins were blue, the sky was white and penguins faded into the stalks of trees. When I re-dream this, when I close my eyes and die again, I will change the penguins to deer, make them a stand of hooves instead of trees, holding still around my body. I will make them deer-brothers without messages of death or dying waiting to be yawned from their mouths. I will change the sky to sunrise and it will bruise my heart with warmth. And I won't wake half-buried in the ground but half-unburied from this death, this hide-and-seek my deer-brother and I are playing in lost woods.

When I re-dream this first non-death-dream, I will wake into almost being alive.

[the third house /// re-opened]

The third house was built on water. I used an axe and a saw. I used a hammer and nails. I used trees cut from the forest surrounding this lake. The surface was stilled. I stood on it and made the house as I had before. Windows, walls. But this third version of the third house was made to fall to the bottom without me, a house only for fish to be consumed in.

I made a chimney for the snow. I made gutters for the rain. I built doorways front and back, and I left the ceiling open, for all the ways fish can school.

In these woods, building a third house for the third time, a house only for fish, is a way of saying *I have nothing left to offer*.

I woke into a death-dream. When I sleep I die.

My deer-brother met me here, in these lost woods, was standing above me when I woke. He was holding a message, a black dot on white paper. I do not believe my brother. I do not believe in my death. He is in hiding, losing himself in these woods so deep I cannot find him.

Fish swim through the windows, through the doorways and the left-open ceiling of this third house. Fish fin through and then pause as in mimicry of furniture, the third version of this third house entirely without interior walls, the fish only pretending. These fish who long to be my brothers, who want to learn my voice, this antler-call, all of them so deer-less that their extended-out brotherhood is gill-laughable. I hear the fish whispering with their mouths, *Brother*, but my retort is lost in the water-logged walls sunk down in this lake.

In these woods, fish are not brothers, and I raise this third house as a net, scooping with it the fish who don't bail through the left-open windows, through the doorways that spill lake back into lake. These pretend-brothers hiding deer-intentions in their bellies, using their scales as camouflage, these fish made to open up in my hands, as eager to disbelieve in their own deaths as I am in mine.

In these woods, I have a knife to gut with, but only when I dream it.

My brother was a deer, his hooves running next to mine, next to the river, in a forest that was our childhood. We were a brother-herd, a path of deer-tails moving. And in that river, these same fish swam, holding still against the current, bodies beneath amber water. In these woods, where I am lost, the fish in this lake, with all of their jealousy, they say up and out of the water *You are dying*, peeling back my ribs with the constant gill-refrains of a brother-tongue.

In these woods, I have a deer-brother to find, a death to dismiss, a purgatory to conquer.

In these woods, I gut.

The fish squirm and wither, squealing fish-death laughter or weeping as my knife forfeits their scales. Inside of the fish I do not find my deer-brother, though in one, for a moment, I think I see him faintly in the fish-blood, but it is only a painting of a city where I never lived, and my brother is not inside of it, and there is no fish-bone message to tell me where he is hiding.

In these woods, I bury the third house in fish scales and innards, fish-bones and empty calling. In these woods, this third version of this third house is drying on the lake's shore, covered in scales.

This third house is a blooming flower made of dying fish, a pyre of missing brother-deer, my staving off death for another day.

[the second bear /// re-split]

Inside the fourth house was a second bear, and it was in the second bear's belly that I found the brightest colors and a way to paint on the walls of a dark cave.

In these woods, my voice is a grain of sound in a muted lake.

In these woods, I am told to die.

The bear rambled into this fourth house, built inside of a mountain, in a cave I made by lifting every stone out and down its side. I made a recess, built the house of cave walls and cavity-darkness, and the bear came looking for dreams.

The bear smiled sharp teeth, and I swung wide with my knife, bear spilling out on a cave floor. Its breathing slowed then stopped, mine elevated. This was inside of a mountain, in my fourth house, where I wanted to dream of love but instead curled beneath death-blankets made by my brother's deer-daughters. This bear, this furred hulk of forest, slowly bleeding into the tunneled-darkness.

In these woods, I dream of living.

I imagine stringed music. I imagine sunset. I imagine my brother standing deer-close to me, his palm on my chest, saying *Hold on Brother*.

In these lost woods, where I woke to a death-dream, my deer-brother was standing over me holding a message of death, and so I began building and burning houses, my disbelief in words.

In these woods, I refuse to die.

As the cut bear drifted, I whispered in his ear *You are not a brother*, its bulk shifting as if drowning in this cave's black.

In these woods, I can no longer see. I am only death-dreaming. My deer-brother dug into the forest, hiding amongst its trees and boughs. My deer-brother river-fast, not wanting to see me as I am.

In these woods I am searching for a word amongst all other words, and even a deer-brother or a sense of longing is not enough to stave off death.

In these woods, a death-dream is a dream where the dead are living.

I have walked these trees to their edges, and beyond it there is only the repetition of forest, the constant of branches, the ash-scatter of houses, all of them built and burned in an attempt to cheat living, to refute death, smoke pluming on a mirrored-horizon where one house becomes two and three and four, where I am the only out-in-the-open deer.

In these woods, where a bear spills and I whisper words.

I will not go gently.

On the cave wall of a fourth house in a forest without end, my deer-brother is inside of it all, hiding as only a deer-brother can, waiting out this dying. He will not surface. I will stay here alone, opening up animals, searching for our lost brotherhood, until death comes.

In these woods, where a bear is words that cave.

In these woods, where I am lost.

Brother, open me up. I am begging you.

[the second non-death-dream /// re-dreamt]

When I woke my brother was standing over me, a message in his hands, my death in a black dot on a white sky. My deer-brother, his hooves motionless. I looked at the black spot and then back to my deer-brother who was by then only a fleck of white tail disappearing into trees, and I was on my back, hoping only to rise again.

This is a death-dream, when we wake to purgatory, when there are woods that look like the woods of our childhood but deceitful, when there is a river we followed as deer-brothers, as herd-children, but now running in loneliness, one brother looking to hide and another calling for answers.

In these woods, to sleep is death, and I refuse to die.

My brother, his deer-face, he didn't want to give me death, to deliver my dying, but someone needed to say *Dear Brother, you are dying.* Our mother and father have already left, so there is only this deer-brother and a river, and the river only ever babbles.

In these woods, *brother* means *burden.*

I search out my deer-brother because he can withdraw the message, refute my death with new words. When we were deer-children, running down this river, and the river broke out of the woods and towards the meadows and cities beyond, my brother said *I do not believe in cities*, and so the cities disappeared into the distance. My deer-brother the magician, my deer-brother the only brother I have ever known.

In these woods, his ten daughters draw death-blankets up to my chin, their deer-daughter arms as white as tails. They sing a song of our deer-childhood, when we were still brothers, a song that carries through brothers, a melody of blood-lining. I sleep and I re-dream the second non-death-dream.

There is a beach, wide with sand. There is a tumbling ocean. The water is blue-green and the sky bright. There are no people along the shore, only one deer-brother at the end of the curving line between sand and sea, his deer-body facing away from me, his head pivoted back, his entire deer-being as still as the antlered sky.

I yell *Deer-brother* down the sand, towards his frozen figure, but he does not move.

There is a scent in the air of this non-death-dream, and I am reminded of rivers, of running. This non-death-dream does not smell of salted ocean but of dirt-floored woods, the musk of light raking through pine-boughs.

Dear Brother, Wait.

I speak but no words suffice. He hears but turns away, heading farther down the shore, further out into the distance, a deer-city disappearing.

I wake into my death-dream, to this constant purgatory, to the feeling of falling downward, to the sinking beneath forest-skin, to death-blankets wrapped lovingly around my body, to no other living left. I want to find my brother but I will not. I want to stay alive but there is no longer life. I want to dream but there is only death. I whisper *Brother*, and the sound turns into wind, slipping from my deer-face, a heart exiting a body.

[the fourth house /// re-burned]

I built the fourth inside of a mountain, in a cave I carved out, moving every stone from its mouth like teeth from a jawline. There was sound but it was only wind tinged with screaming, the second bear burning inside. I had already opened up this second bear, made of him red paint I used to liven up the darkness of the walls, but he was still alive when I burned down the rest, when I laid out my deer-name on the floor and lit it up, waiting for smoke to push me out.

In these woods, loss and being lost are altogether different.

I stood outside of the fourth house, watching the cave-mouth smolder, smoke rising up above these lost woods, the fear of loneliness a silence already passed. I looked down on the deer-valley, the herd-river running, but there were only trees and foxes, pretend-brothers and birds, fish beneath amber river-water. There was no deer-brother in any of this, and the branches wavered in wind.

The fourth house walls collapsed on themselves, and the cave returned to the mountain, filled in with new stones, blackened ash and soot left in an empty belly, in a hollow moment of mountainside.

In these woods, death is quiet loss.

In these woods, I am a deer-brother without a brother.

The smoke goes to the sky and the sky stays where it is. I walk down the mountain. I breathe one last breath of smoke. I hold the horizon where it is and I walk until I overtake it, but beyond the horizon is the same forest I am trapped in, the same mountain-arms I started from, the same glacier-moving I have felt beneath my feet, and I am again where I was. I am on the side of this world, I am back where the smoke serpents upward, I am building and burning again, the second bear dying and then dying again, painted words on the stretch of cave I made to hide my sorrow.

There are no words to tell what purgatory is.

In these woods, I make houses as lures, hoping to hook my deer-brother back to me. He can take this death away. He can hold the message to his chest until it seeps through his ribs, until there is no dying left, until it is only deer-brothers and an endless river to run beside.

There is no solitude in death, no solace.

Dear Brother, Where have you gone?

Dear Brother, Why did you leave me here?

Deer-brother, I am lost.

There is nothing left but to walk, to end up at the start again, to rebuild and re-burn, to re-dream.

In these woods there is only always the moving on.

[the third non-death-dream /// re-dreamt]

Us deer-brothers, when we were children, we stood next to one another and watched the shadows of two deer turn into one, and the way my brother's antlers stood as a crown.

In these woods, where we were a herd running down a river.

When I woke, my brother was standing above me holding a white paper with a black dot. The black dot meant death. When I looked up my deer-brother was no longer there, and I was left to live a death-dream.

In these woods, sleeping is pretending to dream and a death-dream is the loss of living, is a purgatory.

My deer-brother is there in the treeline, watching me build and burn houses in all these failed attempts to signal him back. The foxes came and I destroyed them. One I burned and one I skinned. The bears came and I destroyed them. One I burned and one I spilled. The fish came and I gutted them. Birds came and I lit fire to their feathers, sent them to the sky with bright tails. I was searching for a brother, a tiny deer hidden in fox fur, fox hearts, bear lungs and heads, fish scales and burning bird bones. Seven houses built and burned, seven sets of walls in mountains in skies in lakes in meadows. Seven moments when I wished for a deer-brother to return and nothing happened but fire and flame.

In these woods, I start to believe in death.

Smoke raises to the sky and I cover my body in honey, lay in the open space, wait for the bears to come.

In these woods, an end is an end. This is how the end begins.

[the fourth daughter]

The fourth daughter was made of snow and ice, of glacier, and she fell as deeply as death-blankets in these woods, where I am starving for a brother.

I am a deer, and there is no end to a river that runs. Beyond the sun, where the river seems to go, there is only more sun and more river, until the whole landscape gains back on itself and I am deer-standing where I started, brother-less in lost woods.

This fourth daughter was impervious to sun. She would not melt. This fourth daughter was not the tears she would have shed. This fourth daughter was the daughter I would have had if I could have pretended longer.

In these woods, I still do not love as a deer should.

Glacier I call to her.

In these woods, where my voice echoes.

There was a woman who held me when I was still in deer-youth, and she did her best to remain with a wavering man. We met in a forest. We ate dinner beneath a waterfall. We watched the sun go down through the skin of a window. She rubbed my temples and watched my eyes. There were nights on nights. There were days. There was a river. We were engaged. She pretended or tried to ignore what was the deer-inside of me. We did not make it. There was no way to sustain this. There was more deer-complaint in my heart than there was water in the river running, where my brother and I used to chase our antler-shadows over the forest's dirty floor.

Deer brothers on deer brothers.

In these woods, there is always a river, but the river is no longer the river we chased as children. This is a river of lost woods, where I am slanted towards death and there is this fourth daughter who denies her existence.

The fourth daughter calls to me *Father* and I don't know what to say. I wanted a daughter, I wanted love. I wanted to pretend woman-love for as long as I could, until we were married and there was a deer-daughter I would hold to my body, imagining music in our ears, imagining stars above a deer-river, showing my deer-brother's daughters their cousin-herd, newly begun, teaching my deer-daughter's how they can make of their antlers one shadow, because we come from the same melody, deer-daughters and cousins and uncles and fathers.

Instead, my deer-brother's daughters are weaving death-blankets in the trees above me, and I am struggling to hold on to a dream of a fourth daughter, a girl as a glacier, a life I didn't live, choking on this death.

In these woods, before I was lost, I wanted love and deer-daughters. Before these lost woods I wanted another chance to pretend, if I couldn't admit what I deer-was, back then, before I died.

I held the heart of a woman who loved me, but I couldn't love her back. I was not how a man loves, not how a woman holding a man's hand can love. Beneath stones, where I search for my deer-brother, I find only reminders of loneliness. I find small etchings of men. I find coolness and shade but in a space so small no one can crawl inside, the forest equivalent of trying to love a woman when there is only herd-behavior in your veins.

In these woods, how it is trying to explain what others don't understand.

The trees move in wind, and there is a blight coming through the pines. There is a browning that should be green, a disease like a sunset of dying in this perpetual forest, where the woods and I remain lost no matter what we build or burn.

In this forest, where every animal pretends to be a deer, and every brother pretends to want hiding, the dying is only mine to accept.

This fourth daughter, the glacial moon hanging above us, she is everything I ever wanted and couldn't have, but a deer-brother pleading is not enough to stop this.

A woman begged me. A brother begged me. I couldn't change. A river has no stop and I take after rivers, having lived so much of a deer-life chasing beside one. And now, in this dying, I chase another river that has no end, and there is no deer-brother alongside to steady me.

I said to my brother, when he was deer-concerned, *What about saying only honest words?*

Don't he said. *Resist* he said.

In these woods, where the fourth daughter is an imagined daughter, where all of the daughters are imagined deer, where the river runs, where a glacier slides, I am learning to believe.

Dear Brother, This isn't how it should end.

My brother and I are deer in woods, stumbling through a purgatory of trees and river and our opened-up hearts.

My fourth daughter, from her glacier mouth, she asks the questions my deer-brother asked, questions I still can't answer.

Father, Why is this the world you made?

Father, How can we be when you aren't?

Father, I am cold, but does it really make any difference?

In these woods, I am learning what it means to be cold. I sleep beneath the ground, half dirt and half death-blankets covering my body, waking into the death-dream that holds me here instead of a woman's arms, instead of a fourth daughter's cooing, instead of a glacial love I can recall.

My deer-brother doesn't want to hear the echoes of my deer-kind of love, because these woods aren't meant for congratulating us on losses, the times we didn't but should have and then came to die.

In these woods, I refuse death, but the needles are turning brown and they shouldn't, and there is a fourth daughter melting above me, though she shouldn't, and I couldn't hold to the love of a woman who wanted to be a mother, who could have loved me, who peeled open my deer-chest and saw the real heart there, how it was black and grim around its edges, how it was different than what it should have been.

The clouds are shaped like rivers and deer. I run in their skies.

In these woods, chase is not escape.

In these woods, when the glaciers slide, it is dying and not sun that runs over our arms.

Deer-brother, I am sorry for being who I am.

In these woods, there is no changing who we are.

Glacier I call, but my daughter has melted, pooled, and there is nothing left, and it is like she has drowned in how I was or couldn't be, in how I pretended.

[the fifth house /// rebuilt]

In these woods, where the glaciers end and the shrub brush begins, I rebuilt my fifth house and waited for my deer-brother to return.

I was wearing a scarf in these woods, awakened with it wrapped on my deer-neck, and I unwound it from the wind of my throat, and I made of it the fifth house again, rabbits wilted around its corners, all black and flame-startled by the fire snuck in through their eyes and out their fur.

In these woods I call *Brother*, and there is no sound.

I unwind my scarf and build walls. I make a ceiling and a soft floor to curl on. I build a chimney for the snow and gutters for the rain. I leave a trail of scarf-yarn from the fifth house to the anchor point where all of this began, so my deer-brother can find me again, when he is ready to start looking.

I wait in this fifth house, and the yarn makes a quiet I cannot hear.

In these woods, I cover my arms in honey and hold them open to the sun, waiting for bears to eat my limbs as a pine-blight eats the needles. The sky above is blue. There is no daughter here to rescue me and no deer-brother to stand beside this river with, and the honey dries before any bear comes, and the branches break above me in a failure of wanting.

In these woods, I am waiting for death.

I don't want to die, but I have disbelieved in it for so long that it may have come true.

In these woods, once words are spoken, they cannot be gathered back.

The open doorway of this fifth house rebuilt, it baits rabbits, its scarf-yarn floor the kind of lush love a den of rabbits wants, and they pour over the threshold. I lay with them on the floor, pooling in their soft skins, pelts like pillows, paws like resting heart-rates. They come spilling in the windows and make on top of the yarn-floor a new floor where rabbits sift. I grow neck-deep in rabbits and am reminded of the scarf that built this house, of the throat I once used to call out *Brother*.

In these woods, when I call, only more rabbits come, these rabbits pretending to be what they are not, a brother-hypocrisy that pipes in through every hollow of my chest. These rabbits are not brothers. There is no brotherhood in rabbits. There is warmth and lust and sun and texture, but they are no deer-brother.

I say to them *Rabbits are not brothers*, but they nest in me with their rabbit-noses.

The rabbits in this fifth house are furred-waves, and I go to chase the scarf-yarn end like a river running. *My deer-brother* I said, *this is how we follow when we choose to follow.* I wind around trees, through lost woods, trembling and hoof-printing over the dirt floor, watching how the brown needles of dying pine spread out from me in a circumference, how the damage travels, how the trees brown as I trample my way through their branches, how I hear myself calling *Brother, Brother* without knowing I have opened my mouth.

In these woods, where I refuse to believe I am lost.

Deer-brother, What am I learning here?

I followed the scarf-yarn back to where it all started, tripping through these lost woods with an anchor-point to dwell on. I held the end of yarn in my deer-fingers and looked up to see my fifth house rebuilt, the same front door I had walked away from, rabbits piled in its walls and the scarf-end trailed out behind me, headed into the distance, leading me back to the beginning.

There was a banjo of screaming as I pushed my way back into the fifth house, stepping on rabbits as if a floor, leaning against rabbits as walls, sitting on rabbits as furniture and hammering rabbits beneath my fists not understanding how I can be in these woods, dying, how I can walk the entire horizon, never letting go of the yarn-lead, and end up back in this house.

In these woods, I want to flame forever.

I ask the rabbits *Who wants to burn?* and they all make the sound of rabbit-giggling. The foxes I burned and the bears I cut open, they all made the sound of dying. These rabbits they smile when I touch the flames to their fur.

In these woods, there was a fox-skin I wore as a cape and a crown. There was a leg bone I held as a scepter. There was bear's blood I painted with and all the wanting of daughters I didn't father, all the fish scooped up in dead houses and thumbed-open looking for a tiny deer-brother hidden within. There were birds flying on fire. This is how we look for answers when we don't know the questions.

In these woods, where the complications are built into a house of scarf-yarn that will burn faster than any longing I have, I am dying.

Dear Rabbits, Welcome to how it feels.

The scarf-yarn lit and the fifth house walls turned into smoke, the screaming rabbit-giggles tangled in its arms, the smothered embrace of dying as I watched smoke-clouds rise again.

I call *Brother*, and there is only the sound of smoldering.

In these woods, where the sky accepts our blights, our mistakes as ashes.

I walk the trail of yarn behind me, away from the burning fifth house, build it into a scarf again, wrap it around my neck, closing off my throat, saving the words for when I have more than *Brother* to call.

In these woods I walk, and the dying follows me.

[the fifth daughter]

The fifth daughter was composed entirely of letters, held out at arms-length from deer-bodies, hoof-stamped.

Dear Father, I would have looked just like my mother. I would have hugged you with her arms. I would have latched her lips on your cheek. I would have said what her mouth would have said. I wanted to say I love you but you were already missing and I had no body and then I disappeared into a mountain and a river and a lake and a forest. Walk these woods and remember me.

She made a seam in an uneven world, this daughter of letters, the daughters I called to, saying *Words*.

Dear Mother, I am sorry that when the branches reached down into your womb they came back empty, and I am sorry that what should have been an egg nestled in your tresses was instead empty wind. I am sorry I was transitory. There should have been a father but there wasn't. There should have been a mother and it should have been you. If you see a river, a deer standing nears its rocks, walk away until the city engulfs you and there is no memory of trees. This deer-brother you want, he is made otherwise.

There was begging, but it was done in silence, this fifth Daughter holding her breath and the words bundled inside her, the mockery of not being.

Dear River, You run as fast as I ever wanted to run.

My fifth daughter stood above these lost woods, trampled, her letters raining down.

Dear Father, When you were a deer-child, did you wonder where the river would go if you followed it forever? It led me to the horizon, which led me to the clouds, which led me to the sky. I would have had a sister made of mountains. I would have had a sister made of sun. I would have had a sister made of stone. I would have had a sister made of glacial ice. I would have had my mother's arms to hold you with.

The fifth daughter was sweltering with anger, haggard and lost.

Dear Sisters, I never had you, and you never had me. We are trees growing next to each other, never touching. I wanted branches to grow into yours, but ours was a vacant womb.

In these woods, I am only pretending survival.

Dear Mother, Us sisters would have been beautiful. We would all have had your hair. We would have raised these woods as if they were our own. Instead, our father who was not a father is dying inside this forest, and we can only taunt him from the sky. It seems wrong, every way we handle not living, but we don't have any answers. We wrote letters asking for help, but we haven't heard back from you. Have you forgotten about not being a mother, because we have never forgotten about how trees made into houses are like daughters burning.

I am a deer in these woods, and my brother is the only father, the only river not dying.

Dear Father, Have you found your deer-brother yet? We know you've been looking for him, and we know you believe he can save you. He cannot. There is no salvation in messages handed back and forth. These are letters, not love, and don't be confused by our lack of existence. This doesn't mean you have won solitude. This only means there is a mountain and a sun and a stone and a glacier sliding toward you.

In these woods I cannot take back daughters, even if I burn the houses and skin the animals. The ashes and blood are only asking me to accept death.

Dear Woods, How can you house such a man in your belly? How can you hold his deer-love when you should be holding his deer-daughters and their beautiful mother-hair? How can you make us love you still, even as we weep? How is there never any way out of these woods, away from dying, when the trees clearly reach upward?

I burned these letters, their words, this fifth daughter in her paper-shell. There is nothing to be gained from sentences delivered to dying deer in lost woods.

[the sixth house /// rebuilt]

I built the sixth house from every tree in these lost woods. I woke as a faltering herd.

As deer-children, my brother and I would run this river, moving in each other's shadows, making of our heads one set of antlers.

When I lived I was a man who couldn't love women. When I lived I was a deer unlike other deer. When I lived I was running the river to the edge of these woods, and then I would pause at the river's crawling, beyond the trees, watching a city of smoke in the distance, seeing in its catacombs the woman who loved me once, and the lack of love I gave back, and the daughters we never had, and all the secrets deer-hooves hold.

Dear Brother, How did we come from the same deer-mother womb?

I cleared these lost woods of everything. Mountains, rivers, dirt. I took every tree and cut it with an axe and a saw. I chopped and hewed until the ground was peppered with stumps, rank with bright sun uncut by branches. I stacked logs on logs. I rebuilt a sixth house.

I made a chimney for the snow, gutters for the rain. I made the sixth house with every tree in the forest, building one, two, three stories, stories on stories, until the sixth house rebuilt was a tower leaning up to the sky, until it was so wavering and high that I remembered my lost voice and said the words out loud I had forgotten: *I love you deer-brother.*

Dear Brother, I'm sorry it had to be you to tell me. I'm sorry the message wasn't clear enough for myself. I'm sorry there were ever doctors or cell counts. I'm sorry that beneath the woods and the river we ran, there wasn't only unending laughter.

In these woods, I am beginning to find my deer-legs again.

The sixth house wobbles and teeters, and the sky above it rains down shining. There are no clouds today. There is only death and dying, both of which I am learning to understand.

In these woods, purgatory means remembering that antlers are only bone-growth.

When we were children, we ran deer-fast beside the river and there was fall always coming, or it was always spring, or there was a summer sun peering through our limbs, or there was winter-ice gathering on our hides.

In these woods, there is no hiding.

My brother and I ran on deer-legs in our childhood, teaching one another about the coming of seasons, and how we would fall away from everything we had known. My brother fell in love with a woman and the woman gave him ten deer-daughters and those daughters have his deer-face. They are the loveliest herd-women I have ever known.

In these woods, I tried to fall in love with a woman, but I couldn't. There were no deer-daughters in me. There was only a river and a deer-brother and men who stood as tall as trees, faces like pine-boughs, eyes like forest-stars.

When I rebuilt this sixth house, it threatened at every moment to come back down. The wavering in its legs was the deer-heart in my throat, was the waging of war against death, was the fight I had already forgotten or failed.

In these lost woods, I am constantly undone.

This sixth house, with its chimney and its rain, I stepped into its doorway, and I climbed. I climbed flights of stairs until the river was an ever-distant sound and the movement of the house was all I felt beneath my feet. I climbed until the sky was only blue on blue. Beneath me, bees buzzed a halo, bears circled the base, birds dove in and out of its windows and fish swam in its plumbing, slipping like knotted fists out of every bursting-open floorboard.

In these woods, each moment was a moment where I believed resistance was real.

I walked up and up, my deer-thoughts and the blue out those windows, the tan of naked boards sawed and hefted with dying hands. Until I felt the sixth house give way. Until the lean of this structure became magnetized to the ground. Until the sky was whipping by outside the windows and my deer-hooves were slipping on the fish-slick floor, birds spiraling out the doorway, bears scattering below, bee buzz humming louder than the wreckage of coming apart walls.

In these woods, my brother told me I was dying, and I refused to believe him.

In these woods, I am now beginning to understand.

There were women to love, but I couldn't. There were deer-daughters to be had in a different kind of deer-life, but I couldn't live it. I resisted. Until the sixth house of my heart toppled into that running river, until I realized these lost woods are only a projection of remembered losses.

Deer-brother, You were right to hide. Hiding is sometimes all we have.

In these woods, where we come tumbling.

This is a deer-crash and the woods in tatters, animals faded into the treeline, my deer-heart spit out through brother-ribs, the devastation of knowing.

In these woods, I am starting to see what *brother* means.

Dear Brother, I am sorry for hiding.

[the sixth daughter]

The sixth daughter was made of imagination and wind. She crept through my fingers, an apparition. This sixth daughter was the most painful because she seemed so close to me. It felt as if I was holding her. It felt as if she were holding me. Her eyes were the color of sky, her arms cloud-white, her mouth mountaining-up the side of my world.

In these lost woods, when it all comes back.

In these lost woods there is death, and I can no longer run.

I woke in these woods from a dream of living where there were no daughters of my own, only my brother and his deer-children, the hands of his daughters, my deer-nieces, their fingers waving to me, the uncle with antlers, the man who never gave up the river, who wouldn't stop running. Those deer-daughters of my brother, those nieces, up above me in the trees, the sky behind them, their hands knitting death-blankets and floating them down around me.

Dear Uncle, Why was it that you were always so alone?

I woke in these woods with my brother standing over me, blankets raining down. I watched as he handed me a message, a black dot on a white page, and so there was death, and when I looked up there was no deer-brother, only sky and endless forest and deer-nieces crushing my deer-body with death-blankets. What was left was only one brother without another, a river running.

Deer-Brother, I'm so sorry I refused to believe in this dying.

In these woods, the apologies are ceaseless.

Dear Brother, I am forever sorry.

In these woods I walk in circles and there is no way out. I make for myself a sixth daughter, imagined from within, and she walks beside me, she leans in and out of mountains and trees, winds through foxes and bears, rabbits and birds and fish, evolving out of the treeline, and me, only waiting for antlers coming, the lost crown of a brother.

Dear Brother, I refused to live because I was afraid of living. I was not like you, and I couldn't believe in the difference. I couldn't admit what was different. I couldn't live the way I was deer-born or meant to. Refusal and secreting away was all I had left.

I am dying, but my deer-heart pretends otherwise.

As young deer-brothers we would run. We ran the river until it broke towards a city, where people were not deer but sidewalks, where people lived beneath buildings, where the concrete slabbed up their lungs, their taxi-cab hearts, their pointless city-eyes, and us deer-brothers running as if life would never end.

In these woods is where I end.

The sixth daughter is the most beautiful daughter. She is ranging and open and lovely. This sixth daughter, she is the best daughter I could ever imagine.

I call to her, *Imagined Wind* but I hear nothing back. There is a wisp of echo, but it only feels like the smallest heartbeat going quiet, it only resonates because I don't know what else to focus my antlers upon.

Dear Woods, Other than death, I have nothing left to offer.

Inside of my sixth daughter there is the story of men, a deer herd that couldn't make a daughter, antlers that made the shadows of other antlers, men on men who have no womb for daughters.

In these woods, there is endless sky. This is the beginning of dying. This is a forest of regret.

I call to her again, *Daughter* and her winded-voice calls back *Dear Father*, but like my brother, I am already fading into clouds, I am a white tail fleeing, I am a wind myself, sweeping upriver.

In these woods, where I am learning what shame means.

My sixth daughter walks beside me until I let her vanish. Until I let go. I have to let go. She is not real. A man and a man only make a deer herd that follows a river in circles, and brothers are not always the same, and guilt is a cityscape.

In these woods, where we were deer-children, I would not change one moment of our running, of our exchanging secrets, even when my brother said *No*, even when he said *You can't*, even when he said *Try not to*, and I did, but I couldn't change my heart. That river is a river I will follow to my death. I deer-am what I deer-am.

In these woods there is a river and a forest, my brother who showed me my dying, and there are his daughters, my deer-nieces, sitting on the branches above me, their death-blankets so warm.

In these woods, I hungered for new truth.

Before, I wanted to see my deer-brother again so he could overturn his deathly-message, reverse the ending he had shown me. I wanted my dear brother to take back this dying. I wanted to live again, even if the world was tired and the disease so thick inside of my deer-body and all of these trees in this forest. I wanted to pretend more daughters, to imagine living. I wanted to believe in myself again, as a man, as a deer in a forest, as so many antlers in a circle of other antlers, secreting away still all that was me, that I couldn't change, that lifted my hooves.

But now, in these woods, where I am lost and dying, where every mountain is the same mountain, where my sixth daughter is pretend and fades into wind, where I no longer believe in life, I want my deer-brother to return so I can put my arms around his shoulders, so I can weep apologies deep into his brother-hide. I want to make amends for not believing in life. I want to apologize for mistrusting the only other herd I have ever known. I want my brother to see that inside of me there is a river that also runs, and it runs as his does, only in a different direction, but it isn't his fault, and I wrongly blamed him for my secrets, and his message to me was not of death but of unveiling, and I was always, as I always was, a stubborn-deer in a rut of pretend living.

My sixth daughter was pretend. *Imagined Wind* I asked the sky and clouds, but there was nothing left. As with all lies, the truth skies above them.

In these woods is what happens before we die.

In these woods, there are only shadows of loss.

Dear Daughter, There is no apology sound enough to offer you.

In these woods, pine needles flood the floor.

[the sixth house /// re-burned]

As a deer I stand and look into a river never-ending. There is a forest. There are hooves. I stand, antlers raised.

In these woods, my deer-brother is not coming back.

There was this death-dream, and now there is nothing. I was a deer and there was a deer-brother, and we were children running beside a river, in a forest, our hearts beating.

In these woods, where deer-brothers are missing, where there are only foxes and bears and birds, rabbits and fish, pine trees.

I woke in these woods and the message was death. A black dot on white paper, my brother handing it to me, my looking up, antlers shadowed in light.

I built the sixth house because I could no longer wander these woods. I needed a house to rest in. I needed solace or understanding, where I was left to die.

I built the sixth house by removing everything from every-thing. What was left was the house I set foot in, where I laid down, where I curved my legs beneath my deer-body, where I rested these antlers. There was sun through windows, and only the sun and the ground and this house were left.

In these woods, I always wanted to be whatever was other than me.

My deer-brother, when we were still a herd and the river was a river and the woods were not lost, we were brothers. We were running.

Dear Brother, What does it mean that I was born how I was, and you were not?

I rested in this sixth house until the sounds of the world came back, and when I looked outside, it was all and only men, all the men in the world come back as foxes or bears, as fish or rabbits or birds, and they broke through the windows, and they crushed through the roof, and they clawed up from the floorboards and came, all of them, each and every one of them, like lies on top of lies, into this sixth house, into my chest, until I was full to bursting.

In this sixth house, these men came as bears and foxes and fish and rabbits and birds. They came not as men but as the forest stuffing down my throat, resounding in bodies without antlers, with all of their openly wanton hearts. These men, they poured, and I was crushed before any of their weight came down on me.

In these woods, the sun shone.

Deer-brother, Do remember when the world was still easy?

I built this sixth house and men came through its windows as they had in my own deer-life, and I couldn't grapple a way out. My deer-brother's daughters are in these trees, and these nieces drop down death-blankets they have knitted with their deer-hands, and the world goes colder. And the men are a mass atop me, and the want to burn is stronger than the sky above us.

In these woods, this river turns to revelations.

At the end of this sixth house is the end of me. I am moving more slowly. I am suffocating beneath the bodies of non- brothers, of men who aren't deer, of my realizations. I still want to cover myself in honey, wait for the bears, but the air is stiff and they have no interest in what is left of me. I am underneath so much now that I struggle just to invent living. In this sixth house, where a river runs through me.

There was no way to be different. I was born a deer with a deer-brother and I lived as a herd and men came. There was no house tall enough to build and burn, to keep the men out, to keep myself in, to keep all the secrets dark and hiding.

In these woods, where I am dying. In these woods where all is deer-lost.

The men came without invitation, smothering and thick. Men streaming through windows. It was all men tromping through carefully crafted deer-lives, trouncing what was supposed to be. My deer brother said *The river is only a place to follow. You can walk away from it. The river will go on without you.* But I could not. The river is where deer go, there was no other way.

Deer-daughters knit me death-blankets, to put their uncle to rest, the man they saw living sad and lonely and secreted away, unlike their own deer-father, his antlers pointed ever-higher towards the sky.

In these woods, this sixth house, where my deer-eyes grow weary, even the idea of writing back to you now, on a page white except for one blackened space, is too much.

Dear Brother,

In this sixth house, beneath the rubble of men, I light a fire. It starts deep in a deer-body, where the heart is and a river runs out, full of flames and spittle, of venom and spite for living the way I lived, for not admitting out loud that I was a deer in the way I was a deer.

I lit a fire and the house blazed, the men groaned a collective finish, what sounded like joy unmasked. Then here, in this sixth house, the moment of truth escaping my lungs, deer-antlers splintered and broken, men gasping, and our hearts burning down.

How it is to be a deer in a world of men, in a world of brother-loss, in a place where the inside of a heart is a river running in the opposite direction of everything else. Where the magic trick is staying alive beneath the weight of men on men.

In these woods, where fire is truth to trees, where I burn down.

[the seventh daughter]

The seventh daughter was made of deer, thousands of them shaped into a girl, running through these woods, over mountains, a rush of hooves thrusting beneath sky. A girl in herds, a daughter running through us.

I remember what it was like to hold a woman, like a bear cradling a hummingbird. She asked *Do you want to make a child with me?* and I said *Is a deer such a great animal to raise in a world where nothing is shaped to fit hooves?* and she cried until night came.

Dear Woods, The open arms of your forest comfort me in the way only a river and trees can.

I remember that we slept beside one another, this woman and I, her limbs tangled across mine, and the deer in me was swimming, working to form the right moment. Fox, bear. Bird, fish, rabbit. There was honey over her body but I was uninterested. There was no vibrancy in any woman. There was a house in her bones that I wanted only to burn down. There was a house in all female structures that I wanted to light fire to, to watch smoke and burn, so see coat their eyes in smoldering.

This seventh daughter, the one made of deer, she happily hummed over the space of these lost woods, up and over the mountains, out of it all as quickly as sunset, as if she had never been.

I called to her *Deer-daughter* but nothing came back. This was the shortest lived daughter I ever made, but her body was the absolute closest to my deer-own.

I remember nights where I wept for wanting a man, for wanting to be a bear in a deer's world or for wanting a bear in a deer-embrace or for wanting so many of the animals I was afraid of in myself. My antlers scraped wall and ceiling and I remember asking my brother why it felt like there was no daughter for me to have. I remember how he looked at me and his antlers ran with rivers. I remember how I was still in a herd of deer, but the hooves were all running counter.

In these woods, when we were deer brothers and our antlers were still fuzzed, we didn't know the world would change, that one of us would hide and shirk and shrink while the other would make deer-nieces who would stare up at their uncle with black and round deer-eyes smiling.

In these woods, I am awake. These nieces rain death-blankets down on my shoulders, on my chest, my trying to look up at the sky, without energy anymore to move ahead, with only regret left to sort.

In these woods, dying.

The seventh daughter was not, as with all the others, difficult. She was the easiest daughter I could have made. She ran in herds until the herds split and spread, disseminated over the stretch of forest I could not find with my own hooves, and it was as if there was no daughter at all.

Deer-daughter I called, but I was only pretending search. I heard her hooves go.

In these woods, where I have died.

I remember asking my brother once, by the river, coated in summer-light and pine, *What will death be like?* and my brother saying, *For some of us, it will be white light spilling into our hearts.* I remember how the sky was blue through branches. I remember how he was looking away, beyond the edge of what we knew, and I remember how the deer shape of my brother then, in that instant, moved farther away from me than it ever had before.

This seventh daughter is gone, in her place only solemn woods and the body of a deer, all scathed and worn from trying.

In these woods, a black dot on white space, and how his antlers fled before I could fully wake, and how he scattered as this seventh daughter has, how I have been building houses for my brother to return to for so long. And how he hasn't. And how there is, inside of everyone, no matter the deer-frame, the want for what once was.

The woman who loved me loved me not as a deer but as a man, and I couldn't cope with how she was built. The man-hands that gripped her body were foreign stems reaching out from me like trees, uncomfortable glaciers, the combined weight of simple snow breaking all the limbs in its wake.

In these woods, I am waking.

The seventh daughter, made fully of deer and a suspension of disbelief, she ran, and only then did an end seem possible, and there was light coming up that hadn't been, and I understood what kind of purgatory this was, and how we are all waiting to purge from our bodies what we have shoddily hidden as deer and bears and foxes and rabbits and birds and fish. What is under our tongues, beneath our trees, in our roots.

Dear woods, Where do I go now, when there is nothing left for your branches to cover?

[the seventh house /// rebuilt]

In the clouds, I rebuilt the seventh house. I hefted the forest on my shoulders and climbed the sky. I lay a foundation to hold in the cloud-softness. I built a chimney for the snow and gutters for the rain. I built a room where my brother and I can sit when he returns. I built a sun around us.

In these woods, I build and build. I saw and cut and hew.

In these woods, death has come.

I refused to believe in dying, even with my brother's lovely deer-daughters knitting their death-blankets above me, dropping their curled yarn down on my body. Even then I refused to listen to the antlers in this heart, where my deer-river runs.

Deer-woods, There is nothing left to win by refuting you.

My brother was a good deer-brother. He stood tall and straight and held his antlers to the sun. He asked *What would be so different if you ignored all of this?* He didn't mean I was wrong, but that this life would hurt. I should have said *So much* but I didn't say anything, instead just running ahead of him on the river, hoping my brother would follow. He didn't, or couldn't, and I've been searching ever since.

In my brother's house, there are pictures of living. There are ten daughters and a deer-wife. There is the river we used to run, where he parted from our herd. There is a city and everything else outside of us. And there are the woods, framed in his deer-house, lovely with clouds and sunshine.

When we were deer, we moved with the fury of invincibility. When the river ran, it ran with strength. When the forest grew, there were trees going upward. In this seventh house, there is the sound of birds drowned out by the sound of nothing. In these clouds, the woods have disappeared, and only the forest in the walls is left, and I look through them, and out, to sunlight coming through the sky.

I am no longer searching for my deer-brother inside of these woods. I am no longer waiting for his return. He will come, in time. And the bears around the edge of this living, they have all left for higher ground. And the birds are below us now, rabbits on felt-feet, fish swimming. And the foxes have re-skinned themselves, as if my knife was a dream, as if fire was an impossibility, and they play now with one another, ripe in the meadows, watching the rise of clouds beneath this seventh house.

The clouds keep moving upward, and I am raised to a sky going blue-black, and the bears and foxes and fish and rabbits and birds swarm in my heart, lift these deer-antlers up and out. My brother never understood, but will, in future days, how it was to be me in this different kind of a deer-body, how I couldn't change what that meant, how I could only hide it away, until now, where I've finally come to terms. I am dying.

In these woods, where my death was raised, I understand that a secreted life was no life at all.

An axe and a saw. All the woods of these woods. All the animals who are not deer-brothers, all the deer-brothers who no longer chase rivers, or who chase different rivers, or who run beside me even when I no longer see them there.

This seventh house floats about me, until it is indistinguishable from my own body, the sky, the clouds, the white light.

In these woods, where my brother handed me death on paper, a black dot on white space. I cowered when I should have run, or I ran when I should have stood, or I continued pretending until there was no reason left to hide.

A river goes where it wants and there is no way of stopping it. Even a dam is only a momentary lapse. A dam is a dream rivers have when they are waiting to find their next direction. There is no forever in the stopping of a river. There is only pause, and the way we pretend to be a bear when we are deer, or how we wear fox-fur as capes, wield femur-scepters, imagine we are kings of a forest without end, writing messages to whatever is left outside us, hoping this isn't the kind of death we feared most.

In these woods, where I have awoken.

Dear Brother, I am who I am.

This seventh house was more clouds than forest, more wide-expanse than an offering. Inside of those clouds, I stood as a deer, finally proud of the antlers atop my head.

And the end was white light and flame, impossible to tell where I had been.

And the difference between one or the other is, I see now, so absolutely small.